LOVE I

WE THE PEOPLE

NIGHT WHISPERS

SHORT STORIES

BY

HOWARD EVANS

DOUBLE DORJE

Double Dorje
34 Marley House
London, W11 4DJ
UK

ISBN: 978-1-916201262

For my children, Oscar Blue and Elizabeth Rose

Author's note, October 2022

In 2019 I published STILL, a novel that explored a parallel world I discovered during my travels through Turkey, Iran, Afghanistan, India, Nepal and Bhutan.

STILL gave voice to some extraordinary people I met along the road. In LOVE OVER FEAR, TASHI and FEAST, Judith, one of those people, tells of her experiences living in London as the world shuts down in response to the sars-cov-2 virus. Be warned, some of her writing may be triggering.

THE DREAM and LOVE are old stories retold in the context of the peculiar times that started in 2020.

WE THE PEOPLE is a collection of stories that emerged during a weekly writing group I am privileged to share with some inspiring and brilliant writers. These stories found their way together and are dedicated to we, the people. With thanks to Jillian St. Jacques, Seraf Al Zaurak, Sandi Ivey, Courtney Williams, Kathleen Leisure Haberstock, Daniel Alzamora-Dickin, Mariana Alzamora and Ron Louis Mwangaguhunga for opening their generous hearts.

NIGHT WHISPERS is inspired by Professor Stephen Hawking who, as a child, visited the Graves family in Deia.

LOVE IN PECULIAR TIMES

Stories written between 2020 and 2022

LOVE OVER FEAR

Introduction

In 2019 an earthquake fractured a mountain peak in the Himalayas. The event was recorded by the Global Seismographic Network but was considered to be insignificant – a short burst of seismic activity in an unexplored and uninhabited region.

For humanity, the event was far from insignificant; new knowledge spilled out into the world, knowledge that touched many people who had been quietly preparing, without knowing for what. For some, all they could say for sure was 'something happened'. For others, like Judith, who witnessed the event on that Himalayan peak, the consequences were clear.

As much as new knowledge touched humanity, the event also triggered a wave of resistance from those whose aim is to keep people ignorant and asleep, enslaved by an insatiable need to consume and a willingness to sacrifice anything for another hollow promise of happiness.

In 2020 Judith moved to London to take care of the communal home her friends will return to when their work in the mountains is done. This is her story.

I desperately missed Dorje and found my thoughts wondering back to our first devastating encounter in Cannes. Although I returned to my life in Amsterdam - my apartment, my pencils, my journals - meeting Dorje destroyed my passion for the thing I loved most, the writing that had been a part of my life since childhood, since receiving my first journal as a gift from my god mother.

I abandoned Amsterdam. I abandoned my work, my writing, my friends. I moved to Paros, to seek solace in the little house my god mother offered as a retreat. I tried to lose myself in sex - rough and loveless sex, made possible only with enough alcohol to dampen the intuition that could identify every freakish man who would take advantage of a girl hurting like me.

A good man sneaked in, woke me to the violence I was inflicting upon myself. He stayed a while, long enough to remind me of all the good things in life - the earth beneath my feet, the herbs that soothed my mind and stomach, the wild sea and wind that beat against my skin, calling me back into my body, back into a sense of goodness, until all I wanted was to be left alone, to be quiet. I asked him to leave and he did as I asked. He took a boat to Mykonos.

The woman who returned to Amsterdam was quite different to the one who left.

I had no more ambition, no more wish to write, no need to share my thoughts and stories. I took a job in a bar, a village bar within the city, a bar that served more kindness than beer. I practiced kindness with those who needed kindness, and self-defence with those who hadn't yet understood their need. My body learned to dance, an inner dance that showed externally as simplicity, seen only by those with sober eyes. That clean, organised place was a haven for many who did not understand, but were touched by the sense of order they felt there.

My boss was smart enough to see how I was. He understood that he could leave me alone, trust me to look out for him while he turned his attention to his new club on the other side of town. I warned him I might leave one day, without notice, I didn't know when. I kept a bag tucked under the counter. He didn't mind. He accepted that it worked like that, hoped it wouldn't be too soon, paid me weekly in cash, so he wouldn't owe me when the time came.

I never knew if that time would ever come, but I was happy to live my life like that, day by day, waiting, with no sense of disappointment if another day ended and I closed the bar, prepared for tomorrow, rested in the little studio home my boss provided. Nothing belonged to me, but it all felt like mine, until the day that Dorje came to take me away.

He was waiting at the bar when I turned up for work. My boss knew the moment had come. He was like that, had an amazing intuition developed thorough years of serving drunks. He pressed a thick bundle of US dollars into my hand.

"Thank you for everything," he said. "You always have a home to come back to."

I embraced him deeply, this man who, until this moment, understood me better than I.

I followed Dorje out into the street where his car was waiting. He drove us to Paris, to an apartment on Place Vendôme.

It was there that Dorje first invited me to dance the *wind horse*. I already knew how to dance, from working the bar. I already knew more than Dorje. As we danced, he remembered our first meeting in Cannes. His tears flowed and he reached out, trying to find a gesture or word of apology. But he had no need to apologise. What happened then was what was needed - for him, for me. Without that cataclysm, we might have half lived our lives forever.

Now, through all the challenges of our experience, our bodies and minds were strong enough for the love that burned through us when we were together, strong enough to support us when we were apart.

Now was the time to be apart, as Marianne took my place beside Dorje in the Himalayas, and I took her place in London, holding the space for our family as they journeyed. Thanks to Marianne, everything about the apartment was familiar. She'd shown me every nook and cranny, every secret place. She'd introduced me to her friends in the kitchen, the funguses and yeasts that brought magic to her cooking: the *aspergillus oryzae* she used to make tamari and miso; the *rhizopus oligosporus* she used to make tempeh; the sourdough starter; the vinegar mother; the jars of fermenting vegetables, pickles and kimchi.

There was a set of shelves in the pantry just for spices and herbs - some for flavour, some for vigour and some for healing. You could travel the world in that pantry, through so many smells and colours and textures. There were strings of Mallorcan tomatoes, Colombian peppers, black limes from Iran, bundles of herbs gathered from Marianne's gardens hidden in London parks.

There were assorted bottles and jars, crumpled brown paper bags, fine porcelain bowls with lids, all containing some kitchen treasure sourced by Marianne as she cycled through the city.

Day by day, Marianne revealed to me everything she knew. When we'd finished exploring the apartment, she took me down to the shop.

She showed me the collection of ancient and sacred devices used in traditional rites, rituals and ceremonies, some hanging from hooks in the ceiling beams and walls, some contained in display cases and drawers. All were positioned between the street door and the counter, according to the strength of their magical power.

Underneath the counter was a deep drawer which Marianne opened, using her foot to release a hidden catch. She revealed a small but precious collection of objects, each resting in its own individual indentation, each indentation lined with green felt.

A *kangling* (trumpet) made from a thighbone - all that remained of a revered hermit, eaten by a tiger as he meditated outside his mountain cave.

A *damaru* (two headed drum) made from the crania of a twin boy and girl, long anticipated *tulkus* who died young in an earthquake and were blessed with a sky burial, their bones picked clean by vultures.

A *phurba* (knife) made from amber, sky metal and bronze.

A necklace of one hundred and eight skulls carved from human bone.

Two *dorjes* (bronze sceptres) that could be fitted together to become one.

Tingsha bells, joined with a plait of human hair, so precisely tuned that when struck together, the interference shook the building.

Marianne explained how to use each device, saving the damaru for last.

"This one, you don't really need," she said. "It's used to call for stillness but you already know how to do that."

I needed to explore the apartment again at my own speed, to feel my connection with each detail of my new home, to make my mark with my touch and attention. In the dressing room, I let my fingers run through tweeds and corduroys, wools and cashmeres, cottons and silks, linens and leathers. I felt belt buckles made of silver and brass. I held watches, measured their weight, smelled the different metals. I chose one watch for each hand, let my wrists rock backwards and forwards, felt the tiny internal mechanisms translate my movements into energy, stored for slow release, rocking transformed into rotation.

I shed the clothes that served me so well for travelling. I chose looser, layered, colourful clothes, free to dress without the need to hide, without the need to be ready to run. I chose the watch that best suited my rhythm.

I still had so much tension to release after the journey. I needed to soften my mind, my posture, my amygdalae. I had a good model to guide me. The year before, Marianne had invited me into herself, to explore her inner state, given me such a strong impression with which to reset my internal alarms.

Now I saw her as I'd seen her before in a vision, hair unplaited, right arm raised, a golden sword held to the sky.

She was a still point around which the world could spin into chaos, a still point around which the world could be called back into order.

During the first days in London, I slept on the sitting room floor. I slept with the memory of our family gathered together there before. I thought of the boy; reading us, uniting us, leading us into a dance, leading us into a run as a clan through the city.

He ran ahead with a flag raised high, through streets that were once wild, now invisible to people whose eyes were blinded to the wild. That memory, so alive in that space, woke my body to dance again, and I danced. Every day I danced, and every day I danced a little more freely until I was ready to be still.

I took a zafu to the middle of the sitting room and sat. I softened my body; saturating it with my attention, letting my breath settle, gathering sensation behind the back of my eyes, allowing it to widen beyond my body, beyond the apartment, toward the horizon, reaching out for my people.

I called to memory our home in Paris and our final dance together before we separated, before they went to the mountains and I returned to our London home. I couldn't find my people.

A large parcel arrived by regular post. It was wrapped in thick canvas, hand stitched, with my name and address correctly written in black marker pen. The custom's declaration said it was sent by a handicraft company in Old Delhi. It listed the contents as samples of rosewood boxes. I cut the threads and unstitched the fabric. I found layers of brown paper tied with string, and between each layer, tin amulets, for protection from hungry eyes. Inside, I found five wooden boxes and a brief note from Marianne:

"I really hope this parcel makes it through to you. Our driver said he would get a friend in Delhi to post it. We're sending you two boxes filled with precious pills. They're labelled according to need. We helped make them - a long and incredible process using ingredients chosen in anticipation of the days ahead. When you see them, you can imagine how long it took us just to roll each one by hand. Don't open them until the sun has set. We invoked your presence with every incantation and blessing. We all felt you so strongly, felt how much each of us owed to our time with you. There's a box of green tea that Kali wanted you to taste. Another box contains dried algae from mountain rivers. It's to make a soup, like the one we gave to the scholars. The larger box is filled with cordyceps. We dug and prepared them ourselves. You'll need them soon. Dear Judith we all miss you so much and look forward to seeing you again in our home in London. Love always, from Kali, Dorje and Marianne."

That little note touched me deeply with the purity that seeped from every word that Marianne wrote. I still didn't know where they were going, but I was happy to receive gifts from their journey. I took the precious pills to the sitting room, and returned to the kitchen to brew some tea.

From the smell of the dried leaves, to the aroma of the first wash, to the taste of the first brew, I could feel them there, and imagine Kali insisting on sharing that exquisite taste with me. It was a clean, fresh flavour that purified my palate, lifted my spirit, and cleared my mind.

I poured the second brew and opened the box of cordyceps. A hundred mummified caterpillars, beautifully arranged in layers and rows. Plump rigid bodies, yellow ochre in colour. Four pairs of legs. Eyes shiny red. A strange horn growing from their head.

winter worm summer grass

The winter worm was once a ghost moth larva, living life as a root dwelling caterpillar, waiting for up to five years for the perfect moment to become a pupa, to metamorphose into an adult moth, to enjoy a fleeting few days of flight, flirtation and fornication. But these caterpillars weren't always destined to live their own life.

Some were pressed into the service of *ophiocordyceps sinensis,* a fungus that shares the soil with the ghost moth larva, and needs a caterpillar body to fruit and spore.

In order to grow, caterpillars repeat a process called *instar,* shedding an exoskeleton when it becomes too tight, allowing the soft inner body to expand before hardening anew. Around the fifth or sixth instar, its destiny may be altered forever.

If the shedding coincides with the release of *ophiocordyceps sinensis* spores, its soft, inner body may be invaded by the fungus. A battle begins. If the fungus overwhelms the defences of the caterpillar, it will parasitise it and ensure that its next life transition is as a fungus, not a moth.

The last action of the parasitised caterpillar is to tunnel upwards and stop just below the surface, just where the fungus requires. Perhaps its last wish was to see the sky.

But it will not see the sky as a caterpillar or a moth. Instead, the fungus breaks through its mummified head as a bud, and the winter worm lies frozen beneath the earth until spring.

As the earth warms and the grasses begin to grow, the *ophiocordyceps sinensis* bud breaks the surface as a fruiting body in the summer heat. And the winter worm becomes a summer grass.

The last cup of tea was barely warm, but was as delicious as the first. I took the two caterpillars I'd been holding in my hands, and dropped them into a bottle of rice wine. For the lungs, I thought. Of all the medicinal properties ascribed to this extraordinary gift of nature, it was the lungs that called the loudest. I put the bottle of rice wine aside for my own use. I gently closed the box and found a place for it in the pantry.

I thought back to the monastery, to a row of lignified abbots. Each had slowly killed and preserved their physical body with a daily draught of tree lacquer, withdrawing their life force from the extremities to the core. Once the last spark of life had departed, they were undressed, painted and polished so that each had the same sheen as the wooden box in which they'd sat for the last seven years of their life. Each body was dressed in the rainbow colours that celebrated the achievement.

I thought about the last abbot, waiting to break through the dural membrane, to leave through the fontanelle he'd opened in his skull. Dorje delayed the abbot's departure by resting an upturned bronze bowl on his head. When we removed the bowl, the abbot left with such force and fury that an earthquake split the monastery in two.

Did the abbot see the sky?

Did the caterpillar see the sky?

It was evening when I returned to the sitting room and opened one of the boxes. It was packed full of cotton bags filled with precious pills, each tied with a purple string. On top, a note written by Kali:

"Lungs. Inhalation, inspiration. Exhalation, communication. Opening and releasing. Clearing and grieving. One pill each day with a prayer before bed. Fifteen days and not one more."

I opened one of the bags and inhaled the rich aroma: a blend of earth elements and rare metals; berries, barks and ashes; intentions transmitted through mudra and mantra. I spilled one pill into the palm of my hand. Light clay and plant matter, rolled into a ball the size of a small pea.

I took it into my mouth, savoured it with a palate wiped clean with green tea. I could taste Marianne's touch amongst the myriad flavours and qualities. I could feel my heart settle, a little slower, a little easier. I could feel my lungs soften, more oxygen with each breath, their grip on my heart more tender. I could feel my intestines unravel, some residual tensions release, gas rising, a small burp.

I could feel the ebb and flow of the fluid within my spine, another breath within the fluid. I settled into a deep meditation, inviting the precious pill to teach me its ways.

The sun was rising when I returned from the journey. Thin autumn light pierced a corner of the room.

I opened the other box and found it, too, packed full of cotton bags filled with precious pills, tied with ribbons, some green; some yellow, like the autumn light.

Another note from Kali:

"Green: Liver. Restores hope. Renews vision. Promotes healthy anger with a force like an ophiocordyceps sinensis bud pushing through the dried earth on a summer's day. One pill before breakfast for seven days."

"Yellow: Spleen. Settles anxiety. Overcomes fatigue. Clarifies thinking. One pill if you wake up fretting in the middle of the night."

I opened the garage door from the street. My bike rested against one wall, a gift from my old boss. A Dutch priest bike, its crossbar dropped low to accommodate a priest's frock. I asked my boss to send it to Marianne after I met her in London. It was perfect. She was as tall as I, and now it came back to me ready to ride, polished to a funereal black gleam like the Mercedes. She'd added a wicker basket on the front.

It took no more than a few minutes of pedalling to feel the elation I always felt riding that bike. High above pedestrians and cars, back straight, arms relaxed, gears beautifully tuned for city streets. I headed out onto Piccadilly, following park routes and back streets to the river. Then across Chelsea Bridge and through Battersea Park to the stupa. It felt like a lifetime since I was here last.

I parked the bike and opened my Turkish Carpet bag. I took out the *damaru,* not sure if I needed it, but holding it just in case. I called for stillness. No need for the *damaru*. The veils fell away. The stupa fell away and I was sitting with my back to the mouth of a cave, gazing across a wide languid river, to a place where, long ago, a tribe of women and children beached their coracles and followed the pull of a pointing stone.

I could see the place where the badgers came to drink. There were no more badgers, but the path they followed was forever.

I was drawn to a movement in the air, energy streaming upwards from trees across the river, dust motes, pollens and fungus spores dancing in the web of energies. There was something new in the air, something new jostling for its place, too small for me to see anything more than its effect.

I inhaled, bringing a little more awareness to the soft, sensitive tissues of my sinuses, to the nerves passing through the cribriform plate, little buds of brain touching the outside world.

What was the new sensation I felt? An irritation? A slight tug on the membranes at the back of my eyes? I couldn't be sure. I dropped the stillness, boarded my bike and set off through the park for a slow ride home, still uncertain what I saw, still uncertain what I felt.

Over the next few weeks, what I felt in the air that day became more real. I felt a virus, as eager to exert its influence on the world as the mushroom spores, pollens and myriad other life forms and intentions that share the air we breathe, the earth on which we walk, the body in which we reside.

The newcomer's influence was strong and it travelled fast. Unlike a pollen or a spore, it inspired more than a sneeze, more than itchy eyes and a runny nose. It turned its hosts into factories, reproducing itself, using the host to distribute itself far and wide, without signalling even a hint of invasion until too late.

It quickly spread sickness and death around the world. It spread confusion and chaos around the world. It spread a search for healing and community around the world.

Each day, when I went out on my bicycle ride through the city, I found a place - in the street, by the river, in a park, to stop and breathe more deeply, with more awareness.

I could feel the air, warmed by the heat of the blood within my sinuses, travelling into my lungs, an exchange across the soft, moist, blood-rich boundary.

Oxygen swapped for carbon dioxide, clarity for sleep, bright red blood for deep purple.

Inside the sinuses, those caverns within my skull, I could feel the dust motes and pollens, parasites and viruses, bacteria and particulates, attached to fine cilia, stuck to a layer of clear mucous, enveloped and drowned, dribbled down my throat into the acid bath of my stomach. Or coughed up and spat into the gutter.

I could feel the dendritic cells, macrophages, and mucosal lymphocytes identifying, attacking and killing invaders powerful enough to outwit the cilia and the snot. I could feel my immune system gathering information, preparing new strategies, as the stranger pressed and probed my defences.

I could feel danger. This newcomer was not polite. It was not patient. It was not looking to find balance, nor agreement, nor a willingness to share. It wanted to survive as much as I. Perhaps it had already learned from other viruses before it - isolation is its enemy, community its friend.

I felt my isolation and I hungered for my friends.

When I left Amsterdam, I left behind a little circle of friends who brought me stories of the world beyond the Jordaan. Now I missed those stories and I missed those friends and I felt the need to reach out.

My spirit family could no longer help me; they were living in another world, in sacred places hidden in mountains, dancing with finer energies that travelled through light and sound and feeling. I missed them so much. I wanted to be back in that world with them, away from the noise of the city, the noise of so much thinking.

But I'd chosen to stay here, each day more alone, holding the space for them to come back to. I immersed myself more deeply in the noise of the city. I let my attention be drawn to screens in shops and bars, to the radio in passing cars, to people chatting on their phones, to headlines shouting from newsstands. I tried to make some sense from all the scraps, but I felt I didn't know enough.

At home we had a computer, a laptop, usually tucked away in a drawer in the kitchen. It was only ever used for business, to send and receive emails, to do some research, to send a photograph or two. I wanted to use it more, to gather information, to understand what was going on in the world.

I opened myself to the laptop, read the news in many languages, joined forums and groups, found friends and networks, immersed myself in conversations and discussions, watched movies and documentaries, followed exercise routines.

I subscribed to courses and channels, to blogs and podcasts, to so many ideas and opinions, to so much information thrown unremittingly in my face.

I forgot to dance the wind horse. I forgot my tribe. I forgot to sleep. I watched other people cook instead of cooking. I heard the world was closed. It didn't matter, I'd forgotten the world outside. I felt my despair and I wanted to feel it more.

I switched off all the lights and went downstairs to the shop. It was Marianne's suggestion that I practice this skill, and I practiced it well. In the dark I could sense the location of every shelf and cabinet, the table and chairs, the counter, each object hanging from the ceiling and walls.

Marianne told me: "Be prepared - not only for danger, but for a call from above. You don't want to miss either one."

I opened the drawer beneath the counter and bent down, my body astutely aware of the counter edge in front and the wall behind. I took the *kangling*.

It was the first time I touched it and it seized me in an instant, dragged me deep into fear and pain. I was swallowed by the horror concentrated in that thighbone.

I could see the mountain, the snow, the cave, the hermit freezing to death, the tiger starving to death. This was not a good time to be a hungry tiger. This was not a good time to be a man alone.

I heard a call from above. "Just let yourself go." I gave in to the fear, let the pain saturate every cell of my being.

The hermit held out a hand, withdrew his attachment to it, allowing the bitter cold to close the capillaries as the tiger feasted on his flesh, crunching through gristle and bone.

The sated tiger wrapped herself around the hermit and slept, the heat from her body keeping the hermit from freezing to death as he journeyed deeper into himself.

The hermit guided the tiger in her feasting. There were still a few weeks to go before the thaw, before life returned to the surface. The tiger had to learn how to pace herself, how not to gorge, to trust the guidance of the one she ate, to keep him warm at night while he continued his inner work.

Limb by limb, the hermit discarded his body, withdrawing the sense it was his, giving his meat to the tiger, travelling deeper into his core, into his spine, into the fluid within the membrane, into his being within the fluid.

He visited his heart, now beating erratically, struggling to make sense of the loss of limbs, changes in pressure, the leaks and frays. He found the north star in the sky - the still point around which all the constellations turn. He let it touch the sinoatrial node in his heart, calm its agitation, restore its stillness. And from that stillness, his heart found a new beat.

His cerebrospinal fluid, at first troubled and turbulent, now settled. Its rhythm slowed down, like a long quiet river, rising from his heart to his head.

He floated on that river, on a raft made of reeds, into a fluid filled cistern, within the warm embrace of his brain.

Now I could feel the marks in the bone where the tiger gnawed away the flesh. The bone had been cut with a saw, the interior cleaned with a red hot rod, a mouthpiece of silver attached at the end nearest the hip, polished and waxed where it flared at the knee.

Usually, a tiger would eat the guts first, enjoying the concentrated nourishment of the liver and stomach, kidneys and spleen, chitterlings and tripes, fresh arterial blood vibrant with the last breath.

It would spit aside the gall bladder, that sac of bitterness and bile, enough to ruin any meal, enough to ruin an entire life.

The tiger waited, for a sign from the hermit that the moment had come, that he'd gathered everything worth saving and was ready to let go of the rest. The vultures circled overhead; they knew there was more than enough to go round. The tiger sank her teeth deep into the hermit's emaciated belly, ripping through the aorta, almost drowning as the hermit bled out, his heart pumping to the last, until there was nothing left to pump and the muscles flapped like wet rags in the wind.

The tiger lapped her fill. She guarded the corpse for three days and, on the third day, crunched through the skull and let the hermit fly free.

By the time the tiger and vultures had finished their feast, the land had thawed, and beneath the earth, a fungus cracked through the head of its caterpillar host.

I brought the *kangling* to my lips and blew. Its sound was haunting and beautiful, a feeble wailing, a call to hungry ghosts and demons. There was no shortage of both in this part of town and soon, there was little room in the shop to move, little room to breathe.

They pressed against me, pinned me to the floor, sat on my face, sealed my nose and lips with their cold fatty flesh, leaving just enough room for me to barely inhale, each breath tainted with the reek of shit and rotting meat.

They taunted me with my history. A mother unable to love, breasts dry and sour, bottle fed by strangers, left alone to cry, body aching from so much reaching out and no response. All the faces passing by, pinched and judging.

"She's a changeling this one."

"No wonder her mother couldn't love her."

"Don't get too close; she'll give you that look."

Hungry ghosts and demons beat me with my memories until all that was left was despair. I couldn't find the smallest thought with which to counter it. I couldn't find the smallest impulse with which to seek a jewel. I gave myself entirely and relaxed into that dark and dreadful place, willing to be completely overcome, to drown myself in the pointlessness of life.

I signalled my surrender with a sigh and felt the hungry ghosts and demons tear at me like vultures, stripping away the flesh and all its history, disincarnating me until all that remained was flayed bone. Then there was peace. The hungry ghosts fled with their cravings unsated. The demons fled with their anger intact. Their stink remained.

One fine, bright beam of light pierced the darkness, a tiny hole in a shutter. From the place where it touched the wall, I looked at my skeletal self, laid out as a cross, legs apart, arms out to the side. My bones were not brown and dry like the *kangling*, but glossy and pink and vibrant, their marrow core seething with potential, creating liquid life afresh.

The extraordinary blood machine in which I took refuge became whole again, memories of the muscles wiped clean, memories of how to survive, how to fight, how to flourish, built anew from a deep knowledge held within the plasma. I felt a shift, from the personal to the communal. My suffering was swept away. My vision widened to see life as it was. Within me I heard the words:

LOVE OVER FEAR

Marianne left me a book. She kept it in the pantry, on a shelf with a small selection of books on cooking, herbs, and healing. It was leather bound, closed with a button and a leather cord. Under the bookshelf was a small wooden table with an oilcloth cover and two wooden stools. This little room was Marianne's study and parlour as much as it was her pantry. Marianne didn't show me the book, just pointed to it as we chatted.

"Open it when you feel the need," she said.

I unwound the lace from the buffalo horn button, opened the soft leather cover, felt Marianne's presence spill out into the room. Fine writing in Indian ink. Sketches in soft pencil, coloured with aquarelles. Recipes, formulae, memories and aphorisms. I turned to a page at random and found a quote written in Indian ink:

"Know that this house can be useful only to those who have recognized their nothingness and who believe in the possibility of changing."

Written beneath it: "Better washed down with a glass of wine."

I took the bottle of rice wine from the shelf, filled a tall shot glass to the brim. The wine had absorbed some qualities from the caterpillars – the colour of late summer wheat, flavours of earth and grass, mountains and mushroom, the touch of Marianne, Dorje and Kali.

I switched off the laptop, closed the lid and returned it to the drawer. Nothing more for me there. I drained the glass, went to the sitting room, kicked my zafu to the wall and started to walk a slow circle.

I felt a soft reviving quality from the wine, the alcohol loosening my blood, the fungus loosening my lungs, the caterpillar teaching me how to surrender. I walked alone, unable to call any of my family to dance with me.

The wind horse was new, unlike any I'd danced before. I discarded my clothes and danced naked. I felt a solitude I'd never felt before. I raised my arms, danced on the earth, in a forest near a sacred well. I called on her energies and felt her response. I reached up to the sky. I called on the energies from above and felt a wave of love, lightening my loneliness.

I closed my eyes and danced along a mountain ridge, a plummet either side, my legs and feet acutely aware of the sharp rock line on which I teetered. My upper body free to roil the air, to reach for the clouds.

I opened my eyes and danced in the forest, my feet touching dew laden grasses and the soft duff of the forest floor. My head and arms more careful, sharing the air with twigs and branches.

I held a *dorje* in each hand, one pointing upwards and one pointing down, turning in the centre of the room, feet tuned to the wooden floor, feeling for the little knot around which I whirled.

My arms rose and found their rightful place; right hand open to the sky, the *dorje* resting across the palm, stabilised by a gentle grip between the fingers of fire and air. Left hand open to the earth, the *dorje* balanced between the fingers of water and earth. My eyes turned to the left, pulled my brain to the left, drew my head to the left, called my body to follow, turning counter clockwise, turning towards the unknown.

Some attention rested in the stillness of my heart, following the clockwise vortex of the blood, spiralling out through the aorta, balancing the rotation of my body. Some attention was called to the stillness within the fluid filled cistern in the centre of my brain, a neutral place around which my body whirled, around which my lifeblood swirled, gathering life force from heaven and earth.

I turned for a night and a day, following a slow tidal rhythm that seemed to call to me from the edge of the universe. I bathed in the changing light of the sitting room as the moon rose full and prowled the sky. I followed the changing light and shadow as the sun followed her path, and the room settled into dusk. At sunset I stopped and slept.

I took my bicycle out onto the street, into a rare emptiness. It was too strange. I stopped for a moment, reached into my bag, took out the *phurba* made of sky metal, amber and bronze. Marianne told me it would avert unwanted attention. I wanted it in my hand, wanted to feel its power; just in case.

The connection lifted my spirit, unleashed a wild joy in my muscles. My breathing deepened, the air so fresh and clean that my lungs let go of all trepidation. I cycled like a child, whooping and calling out in empty streets. It no longer mattered that I didn't know why, I just followed the call, and the call led me to a hotel built above a sacred well.

I wanted to go in, to visit our hidden rooms, to journey down into the earth, to lie on the granite dome that contained the well. But the hotel was closed, shuttered, not even a doorman to tell me why. I cycled along the pavement, under the colonnade, turning into the park.

I was shocked by the change; the air no longer laced with the smell of burnt oil, but rich with the scent of tree saps, blossoms and sea salt drifting up from the river. Birds had claimed the space and flocked in a vast murmuration, swooping close to the ground, noisier and more fearless than usual.

Foxes and feral cats basked in the sunshine, free from the need to skulk in the shadows while waiting for humans to leave the park at dusk.

The *phurba* touched them too and they were barely aware of my presence.

I found my place under a tree and stopped, leaning my back against its enormous girth.

I could feel the movement beneath the bark, of water drawn up through the xylem, from a long forgotten river that crossed the park from north to south. I could feel the forces drawn from a golden stream that crossed the river from east to west. I felt the love of this tree. I rested in its embrace.

NIKOLA

One thing intrigued me during my time on Paros; the electricity supply. It might seem like a strange question to entertain when you're living in paradise, but that was who I was. I held a Master's degree in Environmental Engineering, specialising in wind energy. Paros was supposed to be the place to clarify my thoughts, before starting my PhD.

That all changed when I found Judith drunk one night outside a bar, and carried her home. Next day, she asked me to stay and I checked out of my hotel room and into Judith's life. Her little house had power enough for a washing machine and a fridge, but I never saw any form of generator, nor any wires outside the building. Judith told me electricity came by cable under the sea. She had nothing more to say on the subject. I guess it was one of the differences that eventually drove us apart, as our interest in each other's body began to wane, and the glue that held us together became brittle.

When Judith asked me to leave, I went to Mykonos.

She told me, "This island's too small to share with you."

She never explained why she wanted me to go.

I thought we were happy together; I'd found peace with her, and freedom from my endless thinking as we tended the garden or challenged the wind and waves with our bodies. I told her I wanted to stay with her forever, forget the PhD, I would build her a windmill.

On Mykonos, the question of electricity returned. I guess I had nothing better to occupy my mind, and it fell back into habitual thinking. Mykonos was popular with tourists during the summer season, and sustained a permanent population of five thousand throughout the year. The hotel I stayed in had electric radiators and independent hot water in every room. As far as I could see, there was no limit on the use of electricity.

One evening, I was talking with my friend Effa in the Gallery Bar. She'd moved from Athens to Mykonos six years before. She told me she was renting a house for the winter.

"What do you do for heating?" I asked. "The evenings are already cold and it doesn't look like there's much firewood to burn."

"I use electricity like everyone else. Firewood is way too expensive to use every day," she replied.

"Where does the electricity come from. From a cable under the sea like on Paros?"

"Really! They have a cable under the sea? No, we have a windmill, at the far end of the island. I haven't seen it myself but people say it's beautiful."

My ears pricked up. A windmill made good sense, more sense than a cable under the sea. Mykonos had a long history of using windmills, traditionally for milling wheat rather than making electricity. Although the other islands in the Cyclades didn't share that tradition, I supposed they used the same method now.

"I don't know," she said. "But I'll ask around for you."

Effa was so much more patient than Judith. The following day I'd planned to take a boat to Delos; I had an appointment with a god. There's a well on Delos where you can throw a gift for Apollo and whisper a prayer in the hope that he'll hear, and not take umbrage at the audacity of the wish or the paucity of the gift. A Bowie knife, bought long ago in Texas, is not a bad gift for a god, and all I asked was a little pointer in life, no more than a sense of direction. My time with Judith had robbed me of that.

I kept my eyes turned back towards the shore, hoping to catch sight of the windmills. Sure enough, as the boat pulled round Delos to approach its tiny harbour, I could see a single windmill on a deserted stretch of Mykonos.

It was one of those tall elegant, three-bladed generators that you see in the hundreds north of San Francisco.

I was surprised it stood alone; I expected at least one other for back-up, in case of mechanical failure or routine maintenance.

I was even more surprised to see the blades were not turning, despite it being such a windy day. Perhaps there was a cable under the sea after all.

I returned to Mykonos after a day in communion with Apollo and met Effa in the Gallery Bar. I told her what I saw - a windmill that didn't move.

"There must be another source of electricity?"

She laughed. "No wonder your girlfriend asked you to leave."

But Effa was kind. "You should go and see it. I've heard it's a beautiful part of the island. Nobody goes there; it must be very peaceful."

Next day, I rented a moped and went in search of the windmill. It was a deserted part of Mykonos, just rock for miles. No houses and no vegetation. After about an hour's careful drive I found the windmill, standing there with its blades still frozen, despite the Meltemi blowing in from the north.

It was a beautiful design; a tall slender column rising from the rock and expanding into a pecan shaped generator pod with three blades. The whole structure appeared to be built of the same metal. It looked like an amalgam of silver and vanadium, perfect and uniform, without a hint of corrosion. It had a silver lustre that seemed to hover away from the surface and a vibrant blue that floated in the air beyond the silver.

Another extraordinary thing about the windmill was that it didn't seem to have any seams or joints or welds. It was as if the entire construction had been extruded in one piece.

I raised my head, following the line of the column high into the air until, at about fifty metres, it bulged into the pod and then opened out to form three blades. I realised, in amazement, that the seamless construction of this windmill continued to the blades.

There was no way the blades could turn and no way the pod could rotate to align with the wind. It was forever fixed, facing out to sea, facing Delos. Perhaps Apollo turned the blades, I thought, chagrin rising in response to this extravagant joke. Although it was worth the journey, I felt disappointed to find that the power for the island did not come from this beautiful sculpture. I sat for a while, enjoying the sense of folly.

On the way back to the moped, I realised I was being watched by an old man sitting outside a small fisherman's house.

"Do you like our windmill?" he called.

He didn't look or sound Greek. He was tall and slim with cropped grey hair and fair skin and spoke perfect English with a neutral accent.

"I like it very much; it's really beautiful. Who made it?"

"You're lucky," he replied. "I look after the windmill. I can tell you everything you want to know."

"You can tell me how it's supposed to generate electricity when the blades don't turn."

"Ah!" he said. "You noticed that."

"Of course, I noticed; anyone can see the blades don't turn. I could see that from Delos and now, up close, I can see the blades were never made to turn."

"Come here," he said, with a wave of his hand. "Come and sit beside me."

I joined him on the stone bench outside the house.

"When you look at the windmill, what colour do you see?" he asked.

I told him what I saw - a seamless column extruded from rock, the colour like fresh cleaned silver. A shimmering blue floating in the air. A shimmering silver floating beneath the blue. And now, as I looked with a little more attention, I could see a strange disorganisation in the air around the blades; little pulses of light flowing outwards, like waves of bions pouring into the sky above a forest on a bright summer's day.

He moved closer, lowered his voice, invited me into his confidence. "Everybody else sees a tall, white windmill with three blades turning, even in the slightest breeze. Don't you find that interesting?"

I answered with a bemused smile.

"Come with me," he said, leading me into the house.

Inside was one large room. In one corner, a kitchen and a small table with seats enough for four. In another corner, a sitting area with two armchairs and a wood burning stove. Above the sitting area was a mezzanine platform reached with a ladder.

Set into the stone floor beneath our feet was a circle made of the same metal as the windmill.

It was decorated with a simple design - a circle etched into the metal, following the outer edge. Inside the circle, an equilateral triangle. A series of lines divided the circle into nine equal sections.

I'd seen the design before, not so long ago, in a book called 'The Enneagram' I found on the shelves in Judith's house. I pored over that book for a week, trying to understand the enneagram types of Judith and me, trying to find a way to reconcile our differences. Judith wasn't interested. "It's not my book," she said.

The man called me from my reverie. "Everybody else sees only a stone floor."

He tapped a curious rhythm with his feet and a trap-door silently opened. He asked me to follow him as he climbed down into the hole.

I climbed down a beech wood ladder fixed to the inside of a tube cut through solid rock.

As my eyes accustomed to the half-light, I could see the rock had been cut in a way that left a precise pattern of two opposing helixes around the sides.

When I reached the bottom, I turned to see I was in a large and beautiful room: the floor laid with light oak planks; the ceiling, a cupola of finely polished granite; three white washed walls hung with kilims, shimmering with a vibrant blue.

The fourth wall looked like a control panel, as unusual as everything else I'd seen so far; three circular glass and silver port-holes arranged as a triangle, in a panel of walnut burr veneer. In each port-hole, a swirling liquid constantly changing colour between kilim blue and Greek sunset pink.

It was such a beautiful room that it made me feel relaxed, at home, in awe and humbled.

Just as I realised the man was no longer with me, he reappeared from behind the kilims, swinging a copper coffee tray with small white porcelain cups and a tall silver, cylindrical coffee pot. He gestured for me to join him and we sat cross legged on a low divan. He introduced himself as he poured the coffee.

"I'm Gustav. Welcome to my home. I look after this windmill. I don't really have to do much as it really looks after itself. But I like to keep things polished. What would you like to know?"

"Everything. Who built this place? When? How does it work?" I asked.

"I'll start with the *when,*" Gustav said, "as that is easy. But the *who* deserves a lot more time and attention. This windmill was built about sixty years ago, to supply the entire island with unlimited power."

I laughed. "I should tell you that I have a degree in Engineering and a Master's degree in Environmental Engineering, specialising in wind energy. This place is very special and truly beautiful. But I have seen nothing here to convince me that this anything more than a remarkable sculpture."

My reaction seemed to come as no surprise to Gustav. But he pointed to the three port-holes on the wall.

"What you see there, that constant change in colour, indicates that the generator is working as intended. The fact that Mykonos has electricity at all times is further proof if you need it. You're welcome to spend the rest of your time looking for some other source of power but, if you can put your suspicions aside for a moment, I'll tell to you where to find the place where electricity is received at a central distribution point in Chora. And I'll tell you how to find the small metal disk where electricity is received at each house.

"But for now, if you want, I can show you some of the wonderful things about the generator. But first, let's drink coffee and I will answer the question of *who*."

It was so nice to listen to Gustav. He had a soft and even voice and a musical rhythm that made me sharpen my attention to every detail of his story.

The coffee was also very good and seemed to bring a sharpness to all my senses.

"Ethiopian," he said. "My own special roast; ground with cardamom and cinnamon."

Gustav told me the windmill had been built by a man from the north, known to him only as Nikola.

"Nikola said he was born in Austria, but his family were Serbian. He came to Mykonos long ago, when I was still a young man, like you now. He became popular with us locals and, in no time, he learned to speak like a local, drink like a local, and play Tavli like a local. But, although Nikola was sociable, it was always on his own terms, and he would disappear for days, even weeks at a time. Nobody knew where he went.

"Islanders are usually discrete, secretive even, so nobody asked him where he'd been. Islanders are also nosy, so everybody looked, and still nobody knew where he went. He rented the little house upstairs but, when he disappeared, nobody even saw him there. He eventually won the house in a game of cards.

"After about eighteen months on the island, Nikola told us, during a night of serious drinking, that he was leaving. He said he was heading east but he would be back again. He returned about three years later.

"He didn't talk much about what he'd been doing, except to say he'd been to India, Tibet and 'places like that'. But there was a marked difference in the way he looked. His eyes had acquired great depth and there was something incredibly reassuring about being with him. It felt as if he knew the answer to everything, but you had no need to ask. He'd also stopped drinking. He could still beat anyone at Tavli and he remained as popular as ever. Nikola continued to live on the island, but his disappearances were more frequent and longer than his appearances.

"Now, when he returned, he looked tired and was often lost in thought. When he came into Chora, he still gathered a crowd, but he brought a contemplative quiet to the table, and drank no more than a small coffee and a glass of water. When people gathered around Nikola, in a bar or café, it was in complete silence, and yet, when they went away, it was as if they had just passed one of the most important times of their life.

"During Nikola's second visit to Mykonos, I was working in a cafe. Occasionally, he would come in, just before closing time and, when I finished work, he'd invite me to drink a glass of hot chocolate with him on the balcony overlooking the sea. These times were mostly silent and yet, during that period, although I still knew almost nothing about Nikola, and he never asked me about myself, I felt a deep connection forming. It felt as if he was pouring knowledge into me.

"One night, a couple of years after Nikola had returned, he invited me to join him after work. I found him on the balcony and he asked me to take a walk with him. I was happy to say yes. We set off by the light of a full moon, walking around the harbour, and out along beaches and over rocks. As we walked, Nikola talked. He talked a lot. He told me how much he loved Mykonos and what an important island it was. He told me it would soon attract many more people, although they wouldn't understand what drew them here.

"Nikola told me there were many other places like this opening up in the world, where people would be drawn in large numbers. He said he intended to leave a gift to Mykonos, to help the island cope with its future. He said it would be one of many gifts he would leave to the world.

"We arrived here just as the sun was rising and, in the glow of the first rays, I saw the windmill. 'You are the first human to see this,' Nikola told me. 'Until this moment it's been invisible.' You can imagine my confusion and amazement at seeing this incredible device standing here - something nobody else had seen, even though this place was perfectly accessible and was passed daily by many boats.

"I wanted to blurt out my disbelief but, with Nikola, everything seemed possible. Nikola told me this was his last night on the island and he needed me to help him.

"The way he asked, there was clearly no choice. He showed me the dance to open the door to this room. He taught me another dance to start the generator, but he asked me to wait for the new moon before doing it. Nikola said the generator would always supply enough electricity for the entire island.

"He gave me a letter for the mayor in which he explained what needed to be done to receive electricity at each building. He also instructed the mayor to make regular payments into a bank account set up for the keeper of the windmill. Nikola then brought me down here and introduced me to my new home.

"He gave me a book explaining the operation of the generator. Then he shook my hand and left. I never saw him again. For the rest of the day, I stayed down here, on the one hand not believing any of this, and on the other obliged to, as I read the hand written manual Nikola had given me. In the manual, Nikola explained that this generator used an unknown and unknowable technology. Any attempt to interfere with it would yield no useful information, and would render the generator useless."

Gustav put a book in my hand. "Take a look. Excuse me a moment, I have to do something next door."

I opened the unmarked cover.

Things to remember

Coffee. The coffee is from Yirgacheffe in Ethiopia. Roasted beans are delivered regularly. You don't have to worry about payment, there is an arrangement. For the blend you like, lightly roast half a cinnamon stick and 10 cardamom pods. Finely grind them with 150 grams of coffee beans.

Car. The Fiat Panda at the back of the house is yours. Everything is legal. You don't need to put any fuel in it; it gathers power when it's near the house. Sometimes it will be borrowed or taken away for a service. There is an arrangement.

Home. The little fisherman's house is yours. Sometimes people call by, out of curiosity. The underground house is known only to you. I didn't build it. A friend cut through the granite using sound and wind. I decorated the space with kilims I commissioned from weavers in Pirot. The furniture, I made myself. Although windows open to the sea from the bedroom, living room and workshop, they are not seen from outside. Down here, you will never be disturbed.

Travel. There is a room for travelling. It has its own instructions. I wouldn't recommend using it too much. It's a strange experience and, each time I used it, I was left feeling a little more fearful, as if I'd left something behind.

A curious sense of familiarity settled over me as I read. I felt as if I'd left something behind. I called out to Gustav but there was no reply. I carried on reading.

The wind generator

As I young man, I was torn between the wishes of my mother, a feminist and self-taught engineer and inventor, bubbling with ideas and creations that inspired me, and my father who was more traditional, a priest in the Orthodox church, who wanted me to follow his dull path. The conflict almost killed me, but my mother won, and my enthusiasm for life returned.

Conflict found me again, when the government tried to draft me into the army. I fled my home and travelled south through the mountains until I reached the sea. There, I met an unusual man, a master of the wind, who became my teacher. He brought me to this island. He helped me build this home.

It was he who cut through the rock with his breath and his songs. It was he who called on storms to keep the fishermen away when we needed privacy. It was he who showed me how to bend light to make things disappear.

It was he who introduced me to the wise creatures, known as the Vril, who tunnel beneath the earth and who shared their knowledge with me.

What you see in the port-holes on the control panel is a liquid crystal that comes from deep within the earth. It is brought to the surface through tunnels and chambers created by the Vril. These tunnels and chambers constantly adapt to the movement of the earth and the power needs of the people. The Vril shared this technology with me, with instructions to share it with the humans who walked the earth. They had noticed that humans had taken a wrong turn and were burning coal and oil to make electricity, when they could have electricity for free.

They had noticed the humans were unaware of the harm they were doing to the workings of the earth by drawing out the lubricants and burning the carbon ballast...

I called out for Gustav, but received no reply. I put down the book and went to look for him, exploring the cave as I went. I passed between the kilims into a long bright passage with rooms opening on one side and a polished granite wall on the other. I had no need to explore; I already knew this place. The kitchen, bedroom, living room and workshop, all like any typical island house, with white washed walls and stone floors. Windows opened onto the sea. At the end of the passage, a room without a door. Walls of rock. Walls curved, apart from one corner where the walls formed a perfect right angle.

On one wall, in a frame, black calligraphy on hand-made paper, the words: 'Press on through'

Now I knew that on the other side of the corner was a long tunnel that descended deep into the earth, to a level close to where the Vril resided.

There was a room, the travel room, a place to rest one's head, to disassemble one's body and reassemble elsewhere. Now I knew that Gustav would not return and this was my home. I made a fresh pot of coffee and returned to the divan to continue reading the book.

Nikola Tesla (28 June 1856 – 7 January 1943)
Serbian inventor, engineer and futurist.

TASHI

The bell from the street rang exactly on time. With a flick of my foot, I released the drawer beneath the counter, removed the dorjes from their place, clicked them together the way Marianne had shown me. I felt an immediate tug, as the metal engaged with the strong forces that flowed beneath the building.

I deepened my grip on the double dorje, felt an enormous sense of companionship and reassurance as I crossed the shop and opened the door, letting the stranger into my world. She immediately recognised the device I was holding and attempted to soothe me with her presence and voice. "Don't worry, you won't need that, those fighting days are behind you."

Her soothing wasn't enough; I'd experienced too much treachery to give up my protection. I tightened my grip on the double dorje, ready to make the small gesture necessary to call it into action.

"No matter," she said. "But we still need to talk, I'm bringing you important information."

Without invitation she sat at the table in the middle of the shop, put her leather satchel on the chair beside her.

With great gentleness she beckoned me. "Come and sit with me. Keep the dorje with you, but I promise you won't need it."

She introduced herself, but I already knew her name from the phone call I received just two days before. Tashi. Now I could feel how much she suited that name. I continued to hold the double dorje, but softened my demeanour, ready to listen to my guest, a little fearful of what she might say. I sat across from her, my dorje hand resting on the table. Now I could look into her eyes, see their mischievous sparkle, feel the wave of care and kindness accumulated through many lives willingly given in service to others. She was a special one. I felt the honour of her presence.

"I'm sorry," I said. "I wasn't sure who to expect and life has been pretty weird of late."

She offered her hands, open, palms up, in the middle of the table. Without hesitation I gave her a hand, felt her warmth, felt reassured by the loving way she held me.

"Don't worry, your family are safe; I have visited every one of them on my way to you. Strange times are ahead and you need to prepare for your role in this."

I put the dorje down.

"It's beautiful," she said. "One of a kind. Made for connection to the great wells. You'll still need it, but it has another use. May I show you?"

I uncoupled the dorjes and pushed them across the table, now no longer afraid, now deeply curious.

"Marianne showed you one way to couple the dorjes - the way of power. But look, there's another way."

As she spoke, she coupled the dorjes the way I knew and, immediately I felt the pull on the energy web beneath us. She released the dorjes and the energy settled again.

Now she brought them together in a different way, but there was no obvious mechanism cast into the bronze. Something extraordinary happened. The metal at the centre of the dorjes softened and melded and, as they became one, all the structures around us melted away.

We were standing in a clearing. Deep beneath us was a great well. When she separated the dorjes the room returned. She passed the dorjes across to me and showed me how to couple them. The direction and point of contact were precise, but were nothing without the little piece of sky metal she revealed within my energy web, and the inner movement I had to make to call it into place.

"That's what makes you who you are," she said, with eyes sparkling like morning sun on a lake.

"That little gift from the sky lets you reconcile all forces, no matter how strong. Marianne already knew that about herself. Now it's your turn to understand what you really are."

"You mean I'm not a treasure seeker, like Kali and Dorje?"

She laughed. Such a beautiful laugh, kind and respectful, just what I needed to lighten me up to receive the truth she came to deliver.

"You will always be a treasure seeker. It's a beautiful skill and it will always be yours to use. But there is something else. That little piece of sky metal is what makes you truly special. Marianne has it too but not so many people do. You already know your relationship with the great wells. You share that much in common with Kali. You already know your ability to recognise the treasures and gifts of others, but I hear you've already had a taste of your ability to call for stillness."

"Why didn't I know about this before? I could have saved everyone so much trouble if I'd known."

"That skill wasn't needed then and, anyway, you weren't strong enough to handle it. What was needed then was your family coming together."

That was all Tashi cared to offer, and she made that quite clear as she changed the subject. "Now, to return to our original business, the reason I called. Do you have the white trumpet we talked about?"

I went across to the display case near the entrance and removed the conch shell. It was beautiful - rare in that it was right turning; its fine white porcelain exterior etched in a script that Marianne could not decipher. But it was incomplete, carved for a mouthpiece that was missing. It was for this reason it was consigned to its place by the shop door. Beauty without power.

I put the conch in her hands and was not surprised when she reached into her jacket pocket and took out the mouthpiece. "Two old friends reunited."

She fitted the mouthpiece and raised the conch. "May I?" she said with a smile. I nodded and she brought the conch to her lips - not puckered, as I expected, but soft and open, blowing as if to ruffle a candle flame. Her breath drifted into the shell through the silver mouthpiece and roiled against the inner whorls before spilling out into the shop. A wave of peacefulness settled over everything.

It was if even the movement of atoms was brought to rest, and the mysterious quality that flowed between them was unshrouded by grace.

My body settled into deep comfort. My breath settled into deep softness. My thinking settled into deep quiet. That soft rolling breath touched my soul. Tashi and I sat for some time in that warm, tender, liquid, loving caress.

And, as the atoms of all things around us found again their dance, we remained soft, remained in touch with the silence that permeated the space between.

"I'll take it if I may?" Tashi said, and she raised her leather satchel to the table. "I hope it's enough," she said, as she emptied out bundles of cash - all used notes, sorted into euros and dollars. Bundles held together by thick brown elastic bands.

"No, no!" I said, raising my hands. "You don't need to pay. It's so obviously yours and you've already given me so much."

"I'm just joking." Tashi smiled. "The money's not for the conch; the money is for you. Marianne told me that business hasn't been so good and you're going to need plenty of cash in hand for a while."

We laughed together - a moment's joy to lighten the weight of what was to come.

"I'm happy to know you, Judith. Soon, I'll need your help. Troubled times are coming and we will have much to do. Can I call you when I need?"

"Of course," I replied. "Whenever you want. Whatever you need."

THE DREAM

"Do you remember when I told you the story about the dream?"

She rolled to face him; her gaze soft from looking at the sky, their noses just two hand spans apart. "Yes, of course I remember. But what made you think of that?"

"I don't know. The sound of the sea, the rattle of pebbles pushed up on the shore, the craw of a seagull, the memory of our first kiss."

"You're funny," she said. "None of those things were in that story."

"I know. But today is the day he's released from prison."

She kissed him; their mouths too close to resist. She savoured his lips, still slightly salty from the swim. She wanted more. Her tongue licked the sea from inside his mouth.

"You didn't say anything about him being released," she said. Now she was no longer soft. She pushed herself up to sitting. "I thought he was in prison for life?"

"That's what it said in the story. 'Life without parole'. But I've had time to think since I wrote that."

"You think about old stories when you could be thinking about me?" she said, now straddling his body where she'd pushed him over, hands to shoulders, pelvis to groin.

"I am able to think of more than one thing at a time," he said.

"Then how come we never make love when you're working on a story?"

The silence was permeated by the distant sounds of children playing by the water's edge, the rattle of pebbles, his breath. She loved the sound of his breath when he was thinking, the exhalation slow, through pursed lips, a slight whistling in the air.

"Is that true?" he asked, vulnerability moistening his eyes, so they sparkled, a little greener than usual.

A wave of love swept through her and she folded forward over his body, whispered in his ear, "Don't be silly, I was just fucking with you, you're always fantastic. But tell me how he managed to get out of prison."

"He changed. Like me, he changed."

She unravelled her body from his, sat up, drew him up to sitting with her fingers "Changed? Tell me the story again; I want to know what changed."

He cleared his throat and took a few deep breaths, the way he always did before he told a story. He closed his eyes and she felt the subtle shift in his presence. He'd already told her of the place he went; a circle of fresh mowed grass, bundles of willow whips, each one marked with a blade, each one reminding him of a story. He opened his eyes.

"At the beginning of the dream he was lying with his head towards the south west, towards the wealth corner. He knew it was the wealth corner because Master Lu had told him so. Master Lu charged him $500 for that information and a further $100 for the brass spike he drove into the wall. Master Lu advised him to sleep with his head towards the wealth corner. This wasn't easy. Although he pushed his bed across the room, because of the orientation of the apartment, he was still obliged to sleep diagonally across the mattress.

"His girlfriend didn't believe him when he said he needed to sleep diagonally because he was so tall. She could see no change. He hadn't grown any taller, and his mattress was just as long as before. She was smart enough not to challenge him; he already had enough problems without her accusing him of lying.

"He wanted to tell her the truth but was too embarrassed to say how he gave his last $600 to the old Chinese Feng Shui Master."

"Hold on a second," she said, raising both hands. "Why dollars? You said pounds before, didn't you?"

"For the American market."

"Oh," she said.

Now the sound of the sea was softer. The tide had turned and the waves settled into the gentle swell of slack water. No rattling pebbles.

She laughed. "The American market? Since when have you been interested in the American market? And the fee for the Feng Shui Master; for the American market as well?"

He loved that about her, the way she listened to his stories, the trouble she took to be sure she understood. "It's a long time since I wrote it, and a good Feng Shui Master is not so easy to find these days."

Her smile asked him to continue.

"As the dream progressed, his body moved by degrees around the bed, until his feet were pointing towards the wealth corner and his head towards the area of helpful people.

"The transition took more than an hour to complete. This might be difficult to believe, but the dream continued without respite throughout his body's journey. The dream was in real time and linear, not the usual multi-layered kaleidoscope of images and symbols more typical of dreams. The dream was exact in its premonition. The location was as it would be. The people were as they would be. Even the weather was the warm grey drizzle that could not have been predicted from the long dry spell that preceded it.

"I watched him dream his dream night after night. I watched his body turn its half circle. I watched intently from within my dream, hoping for some clue as to what went wrong. When his dream was complete, I would wake up, as the sunrise cracked its light into my tiny cell. Each morning when I woke, I held my eyes closed for a moment, checking the dream, checking to see if something had changed, checking for something that might allow me to wake up and not be in this cell. Each morning, I realised the dream was the same, and I'd have to open my eyes to the same cold brick walls.

"You probably realise something strange. Perhaps you wonder how it is that in my dream I can watch the dream of someone else. But the truth is, I don't watch his dream; I only watch his body as he dreams. I only know his dream because he told it to me.

"A month passed from the time I started dreaming that dream to the day I met him. A month before I knew what was happening in his inner world as his body turned on the bed. I started dreaming my dream the night after Master Lu drove a brass spike into my wall. It was not in the wealth corner but in the area of fame. I paid Master Lu $100 for the spike and for the advice he gave me. Master Lu told me I would gain the fame I craved, but not for my acting. 'One day,' he said. 'You will be walking in a part of the city you never usually visit. You'll go to a bar to drink a beer. You'll meet a man. You'll know it's the right man because he'll say he recognises you. You'll say, perhaps you've seen me on TV? But he'll say no, I've seen you in a dream.'

"'He'll invite you to another bar, a quieter bar, where you can talk in private. You'll go with him and he'll tell you that he met an old Feng Shui Master. He'll tell you what you have to do.'

"As predicted, I found myself in a part of the city I'd never normally visit; I'd been called for a casting. When it was over, I needed a beer. A man came up to me at the bar, said he recognised me from somewhere. I already knew the rest of the conversation and, resisting the temptation to be contrary, I followed it through to its proper conclusion. He asked if I'd join him at his table so we could talk in private. I said he was supposed to invite me to another bar. He said he knew, but it was raining harder than he expected.

"Despite my misgivings, I joined him at his table near the fireplace. He told me he'd been troubled by a recurring dream. The world was at war. The scene was of awful carnage. He saw himself shouting orders and directing the killing. He'd been scared by the dream and scared of the future it seemed to predict for him. He avoided anything that might lead him to that destiny. He immersed himself in a reclusive life, studying philosophical and religious texts.

"When his father was killed by an opponent's bullet, he was introduced to Master Lu by the executor of his father's will, who knew of no other way to free him from the burden of his father's sins. Master Lu told him that he had only two choices.

"He could follow his heart, travel to his homeland, avenge his father's death, connect with the destiny he'd already discerned from his dream. The alternative was this meeting with me and the events that would unfold from it. This would not only free him from his father's sins, it would also free his own son, already growing in his girlfriend's womb, from the karma which his father had yet to acquire.

"The man told me that after Master Lu's visit, he started dreaming another dream where we meet in a bar and he asks me to join him for a drink. When we finish our drinks, he invites me to walk with him. We turn off the main road into an alley.

"A man appears from the shadows with a gun and shoots him dead. The killer turns the gun on me, but it jams. I wrestle the killer to the ground just as the police arrive. Forensic evidence implicates the killer in a series of motiveless murders. A life sentence brings an early conclusion to what would otherwise become a reign of unchecked terror. I'm hailed a hero and, through a karmic connection beyond my current understanding, I guarantee the wellbeing of my progeny.

"The man invited me to walk with him. I was still uneasy because of the change of plan due to the rain. My companion assured me that it was the alley that counted, not the bar. I was further reassured when we stepped outside and the rain had become a warm grey drizzle. We turned into the alley and my awareness of events was curtailed by a sharp blow to the back of my head.

"I regained consciousness on the concrete floor of a police cell where I was charged with three counts of murder, evidenced by the gun found in my hand. My companion was dead and my assailant was commended for bravery by the court that sentenced me to life without parole. On my third day in prison, I noticed a small brass button on the wall. After some hours of picking and scraping with my nails I withdrew a brass spike from the brickwork."

Now the silence was complete, all other sounds submerged by the intensity of her listening, by the intensity of his being listened to by her, this woman who could hold him so completely in the present.

Then she laughed. Not at him. At nothing. Perhaps at the sky. A bewildered laugh, freeing all the energy bound up in her listening.

"But what changed?" She asked. "The text is tighter than I remember, but the story's the same, isn't it? How does he get out of jail?"

Slack water turned to ebb tide. Silence rippled by the rattling of pebbles and the hissing of air sucked out of razor clam burrows by the sea.

"I met you," he said. "And you taught me how to love, and you taught me how love could change the world."

Now it was her eyes that sparkled more than usual and she nuzzled her face in his shoulder and smelled him deeply. "So how does the story go?"

He held her there, one hand soft on the back of her neck and the other on her hip.

"His girlfriend taught him how to love and how to trust. He told her everything about his past, about his father and the fighting in his homeland.

"He told her about his father's death, about the will, how he would inherit nothing unless he returned to his homeland to avenge his father. He told her about Master Lu, and the bed, and the spike, and the plan to free himself from his karma."

'Fuck karma,' she said. 'It's for lazy people who prefer to talk than act. I'm pregnant and we need a man not a corpse. Help me move the bed.'

LABYRINTH

I loved my father for his stern and fatherly love. I loved him for the beauty and complexity of his craft. But I hated my father for the work in which he took the greatest pride - the labyrinth. He crafted that monstrous prison out of sweet illusions, promises and lies. Within that labyrinth of trickery and sleight he confined the thing I loved most in life.

Before he undertook that monstrous work, I ran free, part child, part wild creature of the forest and sea. I ran with my friends, free to sleep where we wished, to eat what we wished, to love and kiss who we wished. My father imprisoned that freedom in his vile tangle of cleverness and illusion.

When he realised what he'd done, how the labyrinth would stifle his freedoms too, he plotted his escape with my brother, Icarus. I realised their plot; to erase the wild, to erase the sister and daughter, to make wings of wood, wax and feather, to fly from the towering walls of Crete.

I tampered with their glue. I didn't kill my father, but I killed his soul as he watched his only son plunge into the sea.

THE LATIN CLASS

"*Quod spirat tenera malum mordente puella,*" she read, her eyes flashing briefly in his direction with the ultimate word. Her lips pursed and her tongue licked her teeth as *puella* danced from the heat of her mouth.

But *puella* fell flat on the floor, unseen by him; his eyes too busy following the words in his book. I saw what he didn't see, and I wished it were for me.

She blushed, snatched her attention back from where it tangled up with mine. She didn't notice his furtive glance as she turned back to the text on the page.

"*Quod de Corycio quae venit aura croco,*" she read, rolling her Rs, eyes flicking between him and me, missing his glance every time. "*Vinea quod primis floret cum cana racemis*".

Now he stopped glancing, his body a little more rigid, his gaze fixed on his book, not following the words anymore. Just fixed, holding back something.

Tears perhaps? Or anger?

"Gramina quod redolent quae modo carpsit ovis; Quod myrtis, quod messor Arabs, quod sucina trita."

Quod myrtis, quod messor! Like crushed myrtle?

Despair? Oh no, he thinks it's me she likes!

I flicked off a Gucci loafer, reached my foot far under the table as she read, as he stared at his book. I rubbed my bare foot against his calf, her side of his calf.

AMBEDO

Morning starts before coffee, with a trip to the baker to buy a baguette for breakfast. "The one with seeds," you say. "Ask for *au grain*. And very well done. *Tres bon cuit.*"

I join a little queue outside the baker's door. I move in quickly and bask in the warm, sweet smell, gazing at a selection of breads on shelves to my right. Big loaves, hand moulded, cut into halves and quarters, revealing cavities where the dough expanded to wrap the space created by a well fed yeast.

Ahead of me I saw it, a solitary baguette propped up in the corner of the shelf. A well-cooked baguette covered in seeds. Brown like a mahogany plank. There was only one customer before me. She'd coiffed her thin lilac hair for a trip to the street to do her shopping. I willed her not to want that baguette, your baguette.

She chose a fresh one from the armful the baker brought from the kitchen. The supermarkets had not yet stolen from her the pleasure of shopping every day for food. She bought one and a half baguettes. No point buying more than you need when you can have exactly what you need.

The girl at the counter served her with a smile. She saved some smile for me. She looked tired from too early a morning or too late a night, but she had enthusiasm to spare for each one of us who stood before her.

Across the road, a fresh fish shop. Boxes of oysters prominently displayed. September, the beginning of the oyster season. Time to remember the ocean, stock up on zinc, forget the last oyster that made you promise never to eat another.

Next door, the cheese shop. One customer, attended with great care by an old man who sold cheese from this little shop on the street for his entire life. Shelves of cheeses, there for a sniff or a slim slice to taste.

A friend who worked in a cheese shop told me you have to chase back the growth each morning, before opening the shop, before the customers see the thin mycelium world that creeps across the floor at night. An army of every kind of fungus and bacteria from every kind of cheese.

At the front of the shop, under glass, a hundred little goat cheeses. *Les crottins*. Goat poops. A hundred names and lustres. Each name written in soft pencil on a paper square. Only two or three euros a piece but each as precious as a gem to the cheese shop man.

Rising above them, a single *Valençay*. I buy it; my love for you symbolised by a truncated pyramid, dusted with the ash of burned grapevine clippings, and a well-cooked baguette.

FEAST

A soft voice whispered my name, calling my attention from where it had softened into the deep embrace of the tree. "Judith? Judith, is it really you?'

I turned to face a young man dressed in a black tracksuit. Eyes familiar, but from where? I couldn't recall.

He removed his mask. "Gregorio," he whispered. "From the hotel."

"Oh my god!" I said, memories flowing back, of Gregory and Griselda, the beautiful young Italian orphans who took care of our rooms in the hotel. I moved forward, toward a spontaneous embrace of a rare friend in my lonely life. But he backed away, palms raised, a little fearful.

"What is it Gregory, what happened?"

On the way to the hotel he explained, about the virus, the '*pandemia*', the fear of touch, the fear of death, the confusion he and his sister felt from watching too much news. He talked of the confinement, the hotel shuttered for the first time in its history, the loss of meaning and purpose in a world now empty of others.

"It was only when there was nobody left to serve that we realised how important it was for us to be of service."

Gregory explained how he and Griselda were asked to remain; their relationship with the hotel running deeper than that of any owner.

"We didn't dare contact your family; we were sure the end days were coming. When the hotel closed, we moved into your rooms; we felt safe there. At least we were safe from the television."

Gregory opened a side door into the hotel. "Now they pay Griselda and me to do nothing, just to be here."

He led me down to our suite and the ancient rooms contained within. We found Griselda; like her brother, no longer dressed in her uniform.

Again, fear restrained an embrace, but love filled the space between us. We sat together in the ancient dining hall. This time there was no food to share.

"I'm sorry," Griselda said. "We ate what was left in the freezers. I'm scared to go out. Gregorio gets what he can, but there are not many fresh food shops open in this part of London."

I felt so happy to find friends in this shuttered city. In their company I saw how much I missed human contact and how, in my isolation from others, I had lost the capacity to even notice. Chatting with them helped me understand the chaotic time I'd spent alone.

"Is the '*pandemonia*' the beginning of the end?" Griselda asked.

I didn't know the answer. But now I knew that human relations were stretching thin, as people gave themselves more and more to screens and devices that sucked them dry, drowning out the gentle whisper of their own conscience with a constant chatter and noise. Now I understood how this human separation made it harder for me to feel my family and friends. Now I felt so much tenderness for Gregorio and Griselda, felt the love of a mother for these gentle young people. If I couldn't embrace them, at least I could feed them.

"I'm going home to make some food," I said. "I'll be back for you this evening. Don't worry, everything will be fine."

I cycled across Hyde Park with joy in my heart, cutting through the quiet back streets and crossing Edgware Road to find the supermarket Marianne had told me about. I wanted to cook a dinner fit to break a fast; food to share after so many lonely meals.

A gentle voice called my attention from where I grazed the meat display, not sure what would serve us best, but wanting to choose meat before vegetables and fruit.

"Can I help you, young lady?"

I looked up and met eyes as kind as the voice that came from behind the white cloth mask on the other side of the counter.

"Gorbat?" I asked. He nodded. "Gorbat the guide? What are you doing here? I thought you came to teach."

"At times like these I prefer a knife in my hand than a book. People are no longer hungry for knowledge; they're already full to the brim. A few of us scholars work in this shop; the owner understands us."

A soft roiling exhalation quieted the shop for a moment as Gorbat introduced me to Malalai who tended the shelves of vegetables and fruits, and Laro who served breads and pastries. Beyond the cash registers, Tashi whispered through the white conch shell she held to her lips. "The moment has come, Judith. Can you cook for us all tonight?"

"And the children?" I asked, thinking of Gregorio and Griselda. "They're vulnerable and afraid of the virus."

"And the children too. Don't worry, we'll eat outside on the terrace."

Before I could express surprise that I had a terrace, Tashi was gone. Nothing left but a softness that saturated the atmosphere of the shop. Now the meal had become a feast.

Gorbat prepared three legs of lamb - boned, stuffed with apricots, pine nuts and herbs, tied with a row of shibari knots. Malalai selected the vegetables, fresh herbs and fruit.

Laro wrapped a pile of flat bread. "We'll finish them on the grill," he said.

Once I'd paid, Malalai helped me pack the food into the basket on the front of my bike and strap my bag to the carrier on the back. She took me into a long and deep embrace and whispered in my ear. "You have a family again. We'll help you in every way we can."

Her love helped me weep, hot tears restrained for too long.

Tashi was waiting for me by the garage door. "I think I need to show you the terrace."

She led me along the street to an alley, opened a wrought iron gate.

Stairs led to a landing I'd seen before, through the kitchen door. Marianne told me about the fire escape, but I'd never thought to explore.

A gate opened onto a walkway that led to a large decking terrace. Along one wall, a summer kitchen, protected by a lean-to roof. Gas hob and griddle, sink and work surface. Shelves beneath, stacked with copper pans. Two upright freezers. Jasmine and honeysuckle covering a trellis on the opposite wall.

In the centre of the terrace, a long wooden table with room enough for twelve. Chairs tilted to protect their seats. Above - the sky. No windows, no prying eyes. Another magical place hidden in the city.

We left our supplies on the table. Tashi bade me farewell at the door to the shop. "I'll be back with the scholars at eight."

I prepared the lamb with the marinade Gorbat described, and unpacked the rest of the groceries, putting the labneh, salad and herbs into the fridge, before heading out to fetch Griselda and Gregorio.

I took the back stairs, excited by my new route, excited by the terrace that now glowed golden with the late afternoon sun. I rode my bicycle to the hotel and waited at the entrance Gregorio had used. I had no way to announce my arrival.

But it didn't matter; Griselda opened the door moments after I arrived.

"I felt you coming," she said. Gregorio followed her out.

"Are you sure you're okay to come with me?" I asked.

"Of course," Griselda replied. "We trust you."

We set off together, Griselda sitting sideways on the carrier and Gregorio jogging along beside. The sun, setting behind us, saturated Piccadilly with a light so clear and vibrant that the empty street shimmered with a rare aliveness that reminded me of the evening our family ran together as a tribe.

I introduced Gregory and Griselda to the apartment, showed them the bedrooms, if they wanted to stay, left them in the dressing room with instructions to take what they needed. I warmed the oven for the lamb and opened the door to the terrace. They returned, suitably dressed for both kitchen and feast. White shirts, black trousers, felt clogs. I found them aprons and we set to work.

By the time Tashi and the scholars arrived, much of the cooking was done, and the table outside was set for the seven of us.

Soft lights and candles lit the terrace and the scent of jasmine and honeysuckle tickled the air. Down below, the streets were quiet.

Gorbat prepared the appetiser - a large platter arranged with a bed of wild rocket, mint, coriander, purslane and dill. In the centre, the labneh, drizzled with olive oil from centenarian trees. Around the edges, sour gherkins, French radishes, capers and Lebanese green olives.

Laro opened several bottles of red wine. "From the Lebanon," he said, and then, breaking into a broad smile, continued. "We have family there. scholars like us; scholars who like to fight as much as study."

At my invitation, Tashi took Malalai on a tour, stopping first at the dressing room, in case she wanted to change out of her work clothes. She returned, wearing one of my favourite dresses. Not one I'd ever worn, but one I'd touched many times for the beauty of the fabric. Walnut brown Venetian linen that caressed her with a life of its own.

We took our places at the table on the terrace. I'd anticipated seating Tashi at the head. She refused, insisted that the place was mine. I accepted and, without further discussion, everybody took a seat, men to my right and women to my left.

We settled into silence for a minute as each of us, in our own way, offered gratitude for the feast, and the friends with whom we shared it.

We journeyed gently from course to course, beginning with Gorbat's salad; a blend that softened the tongue, relaxed the stomach and fed the microbiota - that miniature forest of bacteria, fungi, archaea, viruses, and protozoans, that lived within our guts, guarding the walls of our intestines, modulating our immune systems, regulating our minds.

The lamb, its fattiness mitigated with the sourness of apricots, bathed in the sweetness of innocent blood, pomegranate juice, and the earthiness of roasted root vegetables.

We raised glasses of Musar, lush with the history of the Bekaa Valley, drawn to the surface through deep old roots, concentrated into small grapes that only the passionate can bear to grow. We rinsed our palates with glasses of sparkling Galvanina.

We toasted each other, absent family, friends and fools, with small shots of Armagnac. We completed the feast with baklava, and a Calvados made by Marianne's grandfather.

Throughout the meal, we shared our knowledge in the rarefied atmosphere of companions who knew how to listen.

Gorbat described the skill the scholars used as they sheltered underground, hiding from the hordes, resting on the edge of death, willing to turn either way, depending on the voice that called to them.

"The key was equanimity; willingness to find peace in either outcome," he said.

Laro laughed. "Easier for some than for others. Although I was taught to study, when our people left the valley to fight the hordes, I desperately wanted to join them. But, like the other scholars you and your family woke, I was the only remaining copy of certain texts. The originals of the books we memorised were incinerated when the hordes destroyed the White Mountain."

We paused long enough to be touched by the enormity of those words, of the events they described, of the loss of so much wisdom at the hands of those whose only power was violence.

Malalai called us back from the edge of despair.

"The most important thing we learned - more important than how to quiet our breath, slow our heart, and relax our brains, letting them rest gently on the back of our skulls, was to choose our thoughts with great care.

"We were taught to recognise how much our thoughts could harm our inner world, and how much we needed that inner world to nourish us and protect us as we slept and fasted.

"Each time we emerged from our quiescence, to the realisation that we were buried deep beneath rock and earth, starving, each breath taking us closer to death, as strangers ransacked our land, we were greeted by words of fear and anger.

"We learned to reach behind them, to find the nourishing teachings we had preserved within ourselves, that we could call upon to help us soften again, and fall safely back into torpor, trusting our microbiota to watch over us, lest we all became food for the worms."

The stories continued late into the night, the sky darkening as the waning crescent moon slipped below the horizon. Pleiades called our attention. The seven sisters; that tiny constellation, now at the point that marked the moment when the veil between the living and the dead was at its thinnest. We became silent.

Tashi visited me regularly, either directly or as a voice whispered through the conch. The scholars came every day - sometimes to deliver food via the outside stairs as I slept or danced. I would step out and find the freezers refilled, fresh ingredients on the terrace table, a flower, a chocolate.

Sometimes they came by arrangement, via the shop door, to help me prepare meals, or to take tiffin tins filled with food out for delivery. Sometimes they just came to sit and chat or to join me in a dance.

Most of what I needed to know was in the book Marianne left in the pantry. What was not there was embodied by Malalai. We would sit together in the parlour, she recalling recipes and remedies while I wrote and sketched in the book with the soft leather cover.

Tashi whispered the needs of our community. Perhaps a new batch of bone broth fortified with reishi or cordyceps. Perhaps a little paper twist of precious pills - to clear stagnation, chase away troubling thoughts, revive a flagging spirit.

Sometimes what was called for was aduki beans and rice, sometimes duck or lamb, sometimes fresh young mung bean or alfalfa sprouts. Always, fresh picked herbs.

Gregorio and Griselda had their own rooms in the apartment.

I could leave Gregorio to take care of the cooking while Griselda and I went out on the bike to gather herbs, wild leaves and roots from the secret potagers Marianne had planted in London parks and forgotten corners of peoples' gardens.

You might have caught a glimpse of us, on a Dutch priest's bike, polished to funereal black gleam; me, perched high and pedalling, Griselda sitting sideways on the carrier, sometimes singing, often laughing.

Perhaps you saw no more than the sparkle of a tiffin tin in the evening light, or caught the scent of fresh picked herbs, or were touched by a moment of joy that changed the whole tune of the day.

Griselda had an amazing sensitivity to nature's voice, and nature's joy found her to be a perfect instrument through which to express itself in the world.

It came as no surprise when Tashi asked me to introduce Griselda to the well underneath her hotel.

We lay like sisters on the dome, and Griselda's past became clear. And our futures became clear. And I was filled with the joy of being called to service, always there to respond to Tashi's requests, whispered through a shell.

MY MOTHER'S HAND BAG

I don't remember when the fear began, but I remember as clear as a razor cut the moment I understood it, the instant so many questions I had about my mother were answered. Yes, her bag contained things you would expect to find unsettling for a young boy: tampons and sanitary pads; condoms and lubricants; a can of mace; two mobile phones, in addition to the one she always had by her side.

That superficial layer was not the most disturbing. On the day my mother asked me to look for her prayer beads, with such urgency I thought she would kill me if I refused, it was somewhere deeper, somewhere deep down in the bottom where I found our passports, fat bundles of cash, boxes of bullets, a hand gun, a flick-knife and keys to a car I never knew we owned. And in the midst of it all, the prayer beads she wanted me to bring to her; a mala of 108 small amethyst beads with silver spacers. I was surprised it was there. It was usually around her neck or between her fingers and thumb as she counted her prayers.

I kept my mouth firmly shut as I brought her the mala; as a kid you can never be quite sure about the woman who calls herself your mother. Perhaps, I feared, if I showed too much curiosity, she'd pistol whip me or mark me with the blade.

In that moment of silence, I became an accessory, without knowing to what.

Now, when she picked me up at school, I was a little more alert, watching her back for signs of danger. I would draw her away from gossipy parents and, if anybody asked what she did, I'd lie about her baking skills rather than admit I had no idea.

Over time, I became more confident, more like an accomplice than an accessory. Obviously, she meant for me to know what she carried, meant for me to be curious. She no longer scared me; if she'd wanted me dead, she'd have done it when I was small and easy to bury.

It was my twelfth birthday and we spent it together as usual. She'd been away, but she made it back in time, as she always did. She'd need a day or two to rest when she returned from her travels. She'd stay in her room and send me a message if she wanted anything.

I found her sitting in bed with the mala in her hand and the thangka uncovered. She wouldn't usually let me look it, would insist that I keep my eyes on her and my back to the thangka. This time she asked me to turn and face it.

"*Vajrabhairava,*" she said. "The slayer of death."

Beneath the thangka was a small table. At one end, a candlestick, a silver bowl containing brown rice, and the ash from a Japanese incense stick. *Mainichi Byakudan*, my mother's favourite.

At the other end, a neatly wrapped present with my name on a card attached.

"Happy birthday my love," she said. "Come here. Bring your present, I want to watch you open it."

I sat beside her and savagely ripped off the paper the way she'd encouraged me to when I was young. I exposed a wooden box with a brass clasp. I opened it and found a black hand gun and three rows of bullets.

"It's a Beretta 92FS; your father's favourite. He wanted you to have it when the time was right. You're twelve now and man enough to know something about him. Do you like it?"

"I love it," I replied, feeling the cold, dense weight as I lifted the gun from its cradle

"Your father was French, and beautiful in a way that only French men can be. I'm happy to say, I see plenty of him in you. You don't ever need to worry about your looks. Your father crashed into my life one night, asked me to hide him from the SWAT team searching the building.

"When I cracked open the door and saw his eyes, I couldn't resist. I bustled him in, closed and bolted the door, hid him in the spare room under a pile of boxes I hadn't unpacked since the move. When the police banged on the door, I discovered a power of subterfuge I never knew I had.

"They accepted not to come in, unwilling to disturb the imaginary father I convinced them was dying peacefully at home. When the police moved on from our building, I invited your father to dine with me and fell in love with him over a sirloin steak and a bottle of Beaujolais. He wasn't your average kind of a man. As well as being French, he also killed people for a living. 'No women, no children' was his motto. He brought out the killer in me. I did what he couldn't do."

COCOON

It took me three days to wrap myself in the cocoon. I never knew I could produce so much spit.

I was surprised to hear my mother's voice on the recording. It was years since they told me she'd passed away, but her voice was fresh, bright, singing, the way I remembered it from when I was young.

I couldn't understand why she hadn't told me before, why nobody told me before, why this, the most extraordinary thing about being human was kept secret until the day arrived to metamorphose.

The reason only became clear at the end of my mother's recording, when she'd finished describing the process; how to find the gland tucked deep beneath my tongue.

"Our forebears decided it better to keep it a secret until the appointed day. They thought that if we knew about the metamorphosis, we'd waste our human life, just sit around waiting for the day we could shed some limbs, grow our wings and fly."

I decided not to waste my energy pondering the mystery of that mystery; I had so much work to do, stimulating that little gland, milking up some silk, wrapping my body in the shimmering thread, wondering if I would still dream human dreams as I slept and my human body turned to liquid.

LOVE

It was nine years since she saw that little wooden box. Nine years during which she buried her love beneath the heaviness of an overwhelming marriage, just as she'd buried the box deep beneath other boxes - unopened boxes that contained the colourful fabrics and cushions, pictures and souvenirs of her former life.

Now she lived a colourless life, imprisoned by walls painted in expensive earth colours. The same colours as her neighbour's walls, bought from the same shop as her neighbour's paint by the same interior designer.

Nine years she lived this caricature of a life, hoping to forget. Hoping to forget that former life, to forget that former love, to forget the box buried beneath boxes in the attic, high up in this prison of a house, in an attic above rooms she never cared to visit since she first moved in.

Nine years she lived with a man she'd grown to loathe.

Nine years she pretended to enjoy his company, pretended to be impressed by his achievements, learned to smile a false smile that fitted so well in the world of false smiles to which he belonged.

Nine years she stood by his side, dressed the way he liked, smelled the way he liked, cooked the way he liked and kept their home the way the interior designer intended.

Nine years she slept beside him, although as far apart as the bed would permit.

Nine years she closed and vacated her body so he could fuck her when he wanted.

Nine years she pretended she wanted his child, but killed her eggs with her thoughts, disgusted by the idea of bringing another of her husband's achievements into the world.

Nine years had passed, and nothing he said, nothing he bought, nowhere he took her, nobody she ever met, could clear her heart of the man she loved. The man who died in her arms. The man who dropped his broken body in her bed as his beautiful soul caressed and kissed her as he left.

Now she stood in the kitchen, cursing the latest egg embedded into her womb. A perfect embryo, carefully selected by experts who'd harvested her ovaries as if she were a cow, who guaranteed to take the best of her and the best of him and make the perfect son for a man who believed he had the right to buy everything.

She let her darkness and loathing saturate her womb and drive out any hope of nourishment or love until, as she leaned against the granite worktop, she felt the first contraction and the heat of blood running down her legs. Through the pain and the relief and the satisfaction of seeing blood on the wood of the kitchen floor she knew she could not do this again. She knew she could no longer live this lie.

She let the blood flow free and mark her journey drop by drop through the floors of this home she so hated: past the bedroom that would never see her raped again; past the nursery that would never be a prison to her child; past the guest rooms into which she never could bear to invite a guest; past the staff bedrooms used by the servants who stole her last pleasures, shopping for fruit in the market or tending the plants in the garden.

Each floor she passed carried the stain of her blood. Each floor she passed felt like a journey back to herself, through doors she thought she'd closed forever, into layers of memory she thought she'd never see again. Finally, she reached the door to the attic and her hesitation was marked by a last thick clot.

She'd never been through this door. She opened it, and felt light pour into a room long shuttered within her mind.

As she climbed the steep stairs, she could see that the movers had done exactly as instructed and consigned her entire past to this hidden floor.

On the far wall, away from the pool of brightness that shone through the skylight, stood a stack of boxes, each labelled by her with a different colour. Each containing precious things from a different room: from the sitting room where she sat with him when he first came back to her; from the kitchen where she prepared his coffee with beans bought specially for him from the Algerian coffee shop; from the bathroom where she washed him and inspected him and cleaned his wounds each time he came back; from the bedroom where she watched over him and protected him from his memories and fears, and where he died in her arms. And where, as he died, he taught her how to love.

Without interest, she took down the wall of boxes one by one until she found his box. It was the only one unmarked, at the bottom of the wall, stuffed with cushions to protect another box - never opened by her since the day the police brought it to her.

"His possessions," they said. Possessions she never thought to look for after he died and his body was taken away from her. The documents were found in his jacket and the key led to a safe deposit box which they had emptied of its contents.

There was nothing suspicious, they said, nothing to be pursued - no indication of next of kin, which left her as the person to whom to bring his things. She didn't want to open the box, had no wish to know more about him, now he was gone.

She only wanted to hold him tightly, forever, wrapped in the muscle of her heart. Muscle that still missed a beat each time she thought of him.

She packed the box, along with her possessions the week he died. She put everything into storage and stayed with her sister until her flat was sold. She pretended to be courted by her sister's boss, a man whose wealth could swallow her up and whose vanity would never permit him to see beyond the facade she presented. He was convinced he'd finally won her, as he did with everything he wanted.

She wanted to be possessed. She wanted to be dominated, she wanted to be consumed. Better that than to be flayed alive by grief.

In her bedroom she packed the box in a small suitcase with some clothes, some cash, some toiletries. She took nothing else - not her jewels nor photos - none of it felt like it belonged to her. The cash was no problem - she'd earned that anyway.

She closed the front door one last time, leaving her keys inside. She cut roses and took a taxi to leave them on his grave.

"I'm ready," she said. "To find out who you are."

She checked into a suite at her husband's club, and asked to be left alone. It was the kind of club that would keep her secrets from her husband as much as it would hide his secrets from her.

Coincidence put her in the same room where he arrogantly had his way with her, and she returned his greed with a performance she never knew she could muster. It was the perfect place to be.

She summoned a lover and was happy to know her skill in that domain had not diminished over the years. He was available for her just as he'd always been. She never asked, but she always knew when he'd left another lover in her favour. He arrived on time, freshly washed and shaved, bearing gifts of wine and fruit as always.

A decade had not cost him his looks. If anything, he looked better for the smattering of grey hairs at his temples and the softening of the skin around his neck and chin.

He asked nothing of her - nothing about the last nine years and nothing about tomorrow. He didn't disappoint. He called her back into her body with his touch.

He softened her, moistened her, opened her, entered her, responded to her call to enter deeper and held her like this, free from demands, free from expectations until, at last, she spontaneously let go of the knots she had tied in her womb to keep her husband away from all that was most precious.

And they lay like this until the tears streamed freely from her eyes and it was time to ask him to go.

When she woke, late in the morning, she asked the concierge to book her a flight to New York and a suite in her husband's preferred hotel.

She knew she would no longer be travelling in secret. But she also knew her husband would not force her to return. He was predictable, and would wait in the expectation of her coming crawling back, before cutting her off from everything he thought mattered in life. How could a man like him know how little all that meant to her!

In her hotel room with its views over Central Park, she carefully, slowly, ritually, laid out the contents of his box on the bed.

In the centre was the card he gave her with the contact number of the photographer's wife. In the first circle around the card, she arranged nine rolls of unprocessed film.

In the next circle she laid two passports side by side; his watch; a small leather bag which contained a palmful of gold dhirams; a Byzantine cross made of pewter, softened by the touch of so many hands; prayer beads; a simple bronze key.

The passports revealed two different lands, two different birthdays, two different family names. The first name, the one that mattered most because it was all she ever knew him by, was the same on both.

She called the photographer's wife and explained herself. It didn't take long – she'd been expecting her for years.

She walked through the park to the Upper West Side building where the photographer's wife lived.

The doorman called ahead to announce her arrival and directed her across the courtyard, past the fountain, to the far corner where she found the lift. When the lift stopped, she could see a woman waiting on the other side of the latticed gate. She expected to exchange places as the gate opened but the woman gathered her into an embrace.

"Oh, it is you," she said. "I so hoped it would be. I was afraid this moment might never come. Please come in, but prepare yourself for a surprise."

The photographer's wife opened the door to the apartment and bade her enter first. She followed her in, waiting close behind, perhaps afraid she might faint and be in need of catching.

She faced herself across the hall, twelve years younger, stepping ashore from an old Greek ferry. It was an amazing photograph, taken from a distance, capturing a moment of extraordinary aliveness in the life of a young woman. She was walking down the ramp alone, but all eyes were on her - the boat crew, the stevedores and all the passengers waiting for permission to board.

He was there too, hidden in the crowd, as mesmerised as anyone, yet still able to raise a lens and capture the moment, before he disappeared.

Even though she knew who it was, even if she knew the details, still the picture had an amazing effect - uplifting, filled with happiness, radiating love.

She turned to face the photographer's wife, tears streaming down her joyful cheeks, and heard a truth she never knew.

“You changed his life. You changed so many lives. Something happened on that boat and a wave of love flowed out into the world. Come, follow me.”

She followed the photographer's wife down a long corridor, past a series of black and white portraits, each capturing a moment in the life of someone touched by love.

They sat together drinking tea in a large room, lit by a wall of windows that opened out onto the park. It was part lounge, part gallery. The sofas were arranged in a square around a low table, so that each sofa offered a place from which to gaze at images of beauty and peace and love.

As she gazed, gently weeping, the photographer's wife spoke to her.

"My husband was a beautiful man - pure and kind and good. We went to school together, and I loved him from the moment we met. And from that first moment I watched him change the world around him through small acts of kindness and love. As we grew up, he thought he could bring peace to the world by revealing the truth as he saw it, and he revealed that truth through his words and the images he collected as he travelled. He travelled to war zones, hoping to create a wave of awareness that would stop the human horror. But we began to pay a price.

"Each time he returned to me, he returned with a little less of himself, a little less able to love, a little less able to be loved. And finally, he didn't return.

"I don't know how old Imad was when he met my husband - probably no more than a teenager, yet he dragged him from where he fell and stayed with him as he died.

"My husband wrote a letter, a beautiful letter, to send back to me - knowing he was dying, knowing I would never see him again.

"My husband asked Imad to take a picture of him before he died, and Imad captured everything I loved. I'll show it to you later, it's in my bedroom. Imad returned with help, to the place where my husband died. He removed his body to bury him well. He marked a grave for me to visit and say goodbye.

"That was the only time we met, and Imad told me by my husband's grave that he would continue his work and record the truth and show the world. I agreed to sell his photographs if I could.

"And I could; something deep was exchanged that night and his photographs were as easy to sell as my husband's. And that's how we continued. Imad sent his films and I sold them through my husband's agent and cabled the money to his account. I never looked at any of them - I had seen enough suffering and I was no longer convinced that revealing the truth could make a difference. Then he met you and everything changed.

"The technician at the printers found that photograph of you at the end of a roll and called me to the lab. From then on, Imad only ever sent portraits. I couldn't sell them, but I cabled the money anyway - I had enough for it to make no difference.

"I printed the portraits as they came. In all I received nine rolls and each shot was as extraordinary as the last. I framed every one of them and stored them here. And then there were no more rolls. And then there was no more account, and the money I sent was returned.

"All these years I've waited. All these years I've kept this wing of our apartment as a shrine to my dead husband.

"All these years I've kept this collection hidden - until this year when I suddenly let go of the past, and created this gallery, and watched as these photographs changed the lives of everyone who saw them. Come, let me introduce you to my husband."

She followed the photographer's wife back to the entrance, into the other wing of the apartment, into her bedroom - to stand in front of the portrait of her husband. She stood transfixed - her thinking stopped, her sense of self flowing like love through a mind freed of all thoughts, a body freed of all tensions.

"I don't understand. Imad said they met in a war zone, in a bomb crater. Imad said they spent the night together - a night of shelling and shooting. He said your husband helped him through that night, helped him keep his soul. Imad said your husband was shot by a sniper. But you said Imad took this photograph as your husband was dying. I don't understand. He's clean, he's smiling, he's beautiful, his image fills my heart with hope, with love, with happiness."

"That's true. But this is not how my husband looked, this is how my husband was. This is the effect he had, not the way he appeared. This is how I remember him, how everybody remembered him."

"But how can that be? How could he do that?"

"I don't know how he did it. As you said, my husband helped Imad keep his soul and, because of that, he vowed to continue my husband's work. But my husband was already lost. In the end, all he could see was violence and sadness. He forgot that it was his love that changed the world, and he sacrificed his love for truth. But as he was dying, he remembered himself.

"That's when Imad took that picture. Imad didn't understand until he met you. Your love helped him remember himself and he carried that love out into the world. There is one more photograph I haven't showed you yet."

She led her to another room, a small room that opened from the lounge. A small minimally decorated room; carefully lit, with one chair, one photograph. She sat and gazed at the photograph of her and Imad - young, beautiful, happy, in love, hand in hand, standing on the jetty on Paros, watching the ferry leave.

you
and I
are now two
and with some luck
we'll meet some others
who share our writing love
and perhaps we'll form a team
and travel the world together
sharing our funny little poems
with anybody who cares to listen
and perhaps we'll meet many people
and speak with them in loving ways
and if we're really lucky
they will become our friends
and travel with us
to distant lands
eat with us
hold hands
love

WE THE PEOPLE

I AM FROM…
STONE
WITCH
HEXING
THE SPIRIT OF THE WOOD
BLOWN BY THE WIND
BUTCHER
LOCKUP
HORSE TRADER
A DARK TEACHER
THE VILLAGE
DIGGERS
THE PIANO PLAYER
THE POET
QUEEN
LURCHER
CRABS' LEGS
DEATH IN A TRENCH
KEY
THE CODE
KARMA

I AM FROM...

I am from a family of unknown origin. My grandmother lived in the dark, surrounded by violent images: Jesus with a bleeding heart in the palm of his hand; Jesus nailed to a tree, a gaping wound in his side, his mother weeping tears of blood.

My grandmother was always sitting in front of a coal fire, sucking the sweetness from sugared almonds, spitting the nut into the hearth. She never missed. She never offered us a sugared almond.

Her husband, my grandfather, was dead long before I arrived. I saw a photograph. They were short people. They were Short by name and short by nature. It looked like they lived in a wooden box. My mother said it was a prefab. Lots of poor people lived in prefabs after the war.

My mother said he built chimneys. My mother said he built ships. My mother said he worked in the circus when there was nothing left to build.

I am from... I cannot tell you exactly. Perhaps from Ireland. So many short people came from Ireland, to build ships and chimneys in the North of England. I cannot be sure if my grandparents came from Ireland or their parents came before them.

The history of the short people is not well recorded. Often, they changed their name. My grandfather changed his name from Short to Shortt.

Once, when she was sober, my mother told me he was always running from his debts. As a child, she was sent to answer the door, to tell the bailiffs to come back tomorrow when her father would be home. They'd move house in the dead of night, before tomorrow came.

Sometimes, I am from the north, from Newcastle where they built ships and chimneys. Sometimes, I am from the south, from Aldershot where my grandparents moved, where my grandfather became an electrician, where my uncles became soldiers or spivs according to their cunning. The ones who became soldiers were sent to war and came back broken. The ones who became spivs were broken in other ways.

My mother sold tea and pastries from a van. My mother sold cups of tea to my father. Not at the army base, but outside the Royal Aircraft Establishment where he was an apprentice.

I am from… To look at my father it would be hard to say where. His thick black hair remained the same until he died. He had olive skin. 'Swarthy', he'd say. He had a Spanish name, slipped into the space between his first and last names.

We weren´t sure if it was really his name; it wasn't on his passport. He was a handsome man who wore his navy uniform to marry.

Our father took us to Devon, and it felt like home. Our father took us to Cornwall, and it felt like home. Our father took us to Wales, and it felt like home. 'West is best', is what we used to say.

"But where are you really from?" we asked. "Nottingham," he said. "But we moved around a lot."

I came across a man, long bearded like me, walking on the barren rock, above the tree line, above the grass line, the place where only lichens thrive. Yellow lichens, black lichens, white lichens; each lichen coloured according to the direction it faced in life. And perhaps you ask the question, "But why only three colours of lichen when the compass has four directions?"

This was the question I asked of him, this man with a long blue beard, wondering along the top of the mountain.

"Because the south is too hot," he said. "Facing the sun, there is no moisture in the rock to sustain even the life of a lichen." As he spoke, he turned to face the south and the blue faded from his beard, and the whiskers sparkled white. "And for this same reason the rock facing south is smooth."

He led me on a walk around the limestone peak that towered above all the other peaks on this island floating in the sea. He called this peak the *Puig Major,* because that is what it was. Other peaks had other names but only one peak was the biggest. And the sea in which the island floated was only ever called *the sea*. Because back then, in the time of which I speak, there was only one sea, in the same way as there was only one sun.

As we spiralled around the *Puig Major*, his beard turned from blue to yellow to white. And as we looked at the rock, we saw that the rock was marked in different ways according to the direction it faced.

"We call this rock limestone," he said. "Because that is what it is. This whole island in the middle of the sea is just one enormous limestone rock. And it changes every day. It changes because it is soft and succumbs easily to the wind and the rain and the waves. On the south side, the rock is smooth because the water never stays there for long. But on the north, the rock is riven with grooves and gullies because that side doesn't see the sun, but faces the winds and the rains from the north. Sometimes the winds and rains from the north arrive as violent rampages. Sometimes the wind is so cold that the water freezes and cracks the rock."

"Look here," he said, tapping me with the quill with which he tapped and pointed. I looked where he pointed, to a stone cracked into pieces.

"Water finds fault lines in the stone and, at night, when the temperature falls, the water freezes and cracks the rock."

We squatted together and he taught me how to look with a gaze like his. As I looked, he marked shapes and symbols on a piece of parchment with his quill.

"What is that, that you do?" I asked.

"I write," he said. "God talks to us through nature. I am learning God's language. Walk with me and I will me show you more of what I have learned."

Mother taught us well. By the time the inquisitors came, the house was cleared. She felt them coming two days before the earth trembled under the weight of the horses and the iron carriage. When they were close, she showed us how to recognise the strange sensation at the base of our spine, the tremor of an ethereal tail.

We hid the books and medical instruments. They were heavy. We carried them across the brook, beyond the noses of their dogs and ferrets. We hauled them up into the sacred trees.

We threw medicinal herbs and powders into the river; its waters would always guard our secrets.

We drew veils of dullness and ignorance across our eyes, settled into a simple sliver of our mind, freed from the knowledge and curiosity that would get us killed.

They dragged mother out, screaming for the safety of her children. Her screams could still curdle our blood even if we knew her ruse.

The inquisitors asked no questions, not of her, not of us. Their stupidity thrived on the malice of others. Once a witch was outed, she was as good as dead to them.

They chained her to the iron carriage, torched our home, ignored our tears and entreaties as they took her away.

By the time we reached town, the inquisitors had already tortured mother for two days. They wallowed in their sadism as she filled their lungs with her breath, vibrant with the plague that would rot their lymph glands until they burst in their throats within the week.

We were there in time to see the dunking. She knew we were there, holding her in our hearts as the inquisitors acted out their pointless test. Of course, they couldn't drown a witch; water was our friend. Fire too, unbeknownst to them. As the flames burnt the cords that held her, mesmerising the crowd with its ferocity, she walked free, led us out of town as the inquisitors poisoned the mob with their plague laden breath.

HEXING

In my family we didn't do spells; nobody knew how to spell. We were poor tinkers and spelling had no value to us. But we could put hexes.

My mother taught me how to put a hex before I was seven years old. It wasn't long after that I had to put my skill to the test. I'd been out taking pieces off an old car abandoned on the road side. I had the little tool kit my dad gave me for my fifth birthday.

"This will make you rich," he said as he handed me the tools, wrapped in an oily rag.

The first things to take off an abandoned car are the gauges and lamps. They'd already gone. The seats were too heavy for me to carry so I decided to take the window winders.

The door panel had to be pried off with care, trying not to break the clips, or break the mechanism that lay behind it.

I was levering the panel with a flat headed screwdriver when the kids from the village arrived. They started throwing insults. They were soon followed by punches and kicks as I got out of the car to defend myself.

In my family we put a hex with a smudge of dirt scraped from the sole of the shoe with the finger tips.

I hexed them good. Same hex for them all, hands outstretched in their direction, voice loud like my mother taught me.

"Your dogs will die tonight," I yelled. "Go home and kiss them goodbye." It cost me a split lip from one of the boys before they ran.

I ran as well, but not before I gathered up my tools. But I ran, scared of the power I felt, scared for all the dogs who would die. I liked dogs. We had lurchers.

I asked my mother if there was any way to reverse a hex. She didn't know of any. When I told her what I'd done, she said it might be a good time for us to up and leave. My dad agreed and we abandoned our camp before day break. We had to leave a pile of scrap metal behind; there wasn't enough room on the truck for it all.

I promised my parents I'd make good on the loss. I promised myself I'd be more careful with my hexing. I kept that promise until I was thirty, always finding other ways to resolve conflicts. This time there was no other way.

THE SPIRIT OF THE WOOD

Everybody complained about my kitchen table. The creak cut through every conversation. Some friends even offered to fix it. I think it just needed a couple of screws to replace the missing dowel. I resisted their offers, knowing I had a new table in the making and this one would soon move upstairs to a permanent home on the terrace. Perhaps I'd find a dowel anyway. The creak cut through every conversation.

My mother told us to keep our elbows off the table. Her admonishment bounced off my thick skin and I surrounded myself with like elbowed friends. It was one of many problems I could have avoided if I'd listened to my mother.

It was Kirsty who suggested the table was trying to talk to us. Admittedly, we'd drunk enough good whiskey to leave us open to any suggestion. But Kirsty had a way of saying things, and we would have believed her even without the whiskey

The table was old, a few hundred years perhaps, a heavy burden that needed four strong backs to lift. The oak planks were originally joined together with wooden inserts and dowels.

"Did you know that Stradivarius kept newly made violins and cellos in the bedroom he shared with his wife?" Kirsty asked.

I didn't know, but my mind lit up with such a wonderful thought.

She continued. "The bodies of the instruments were imprinted with their love. He wouldn't sell to just anyone who asked, and he wouldn't let just anybody play. Each instrument was made to order, and each person who played it left their spirit in the wood forever. A Stradivarius could be ruined by one bad player. And, now they cost so much, the player is more likely to be bad than good. Perhaps it's the same with a table?"

"But how would we know?" I asked.

"By listening," she said, pushing her plate away and pressing her ear to the table.

She listened a good minute or so, long enough for us to stop waiting for her words and follow her actions. I pushed my plate away and pressed my ear to the table. The wood was still warm from the plate, and surprisingly soft and silky for something so solid.

I heard the sound of the sea, banging against the wood when it was still the planks of a tall ship. I smelled tea, picked in mountain gardens north of Calcutta.

I saw bales of dried leaves loaded into the belly of a clipper, moored on the Hooghly River, preparing for its journey to East India docks in London.

I felt the fear that saturated that ship. Ahead, for the crew, six months hard labour at best, an icy grave off the Cape of Good Hope at worst.

I was told that our people came from the south, on an enormous ship built of wood, with leather sails stitched from the hides and pelts and skins of every kind of creature. I was told that our people destroyed our homeland before setting sail in search of a new land.

They chopped down all the trees to build a ship. They harvested every blade of grass, every fruit, every seed and every bean to feed our people and our animals on the voyage. They brought cows and sheep and goats to give milk. They brought chickens, doves and rabbits to eat. They killed every remaining creature and used their skin to sew an enormous sail. They dried the meat to eat on the voyage.

Our people felt so much shame for what they'd done that they buried our history deep. They invented other stories. Some said our land had been washed away by a great flood. Some said our land had been swallowed up by the earth. Some said we came from another planet.

My mother said our people invented the wind. I found that hard to believe. My mother said that when our people found our new land, they found knowledge too, transmitted through rocks and plants.

My mother said that in one night our people learned how to write, how to draw, how to make books, how to listen to the language of the earth, how to listen to the language of the trees, how to listen to the language of the sky.

That, I believed, because my mother taught me, and the voice she used to teach me was quite different to the voice she used to bathe me in her love. It was as if that voice came from another place, from somewhere deep inside the earth.

BUTCHER

It was inevitable that, one day, she would ask about my family. For my mother's side it was easy. Irish Catholics, brought over with the promise of work in the shipyards. I don't know of it was true but I liked the sound of it. It explained the fervour with which my aunts and uncles smoked cigarettes and drank tea as they talked and laughed without a break.

My father's side was another matter. My dad said he came from a family of butchers. But I don't remember any butcher shops. I remember land and horses and orchards. I remember a big house where everything was old and beautiful. There was an AGA in the kitchen and the kitchen was always warm.

I remember a chicken run that my dad said was once a tennis court. I remember a pigsty that my dad said was once a squash court. I remember a building lined with tall cabinets with felt lined drawers. That's where the apples and pears, freshly picked from the orchard, were stored to keep through the winter. I remember the sweet smell of fruit and hay.

I remember my grandfather serving us sausages, the best sausages I ever tasted. He called them *dogs*.

He laughed when he saw how many I could put away. That was the closest he ever came to a butcher's shop, as far as I could see.

I remember the stables and twelve trotting horses. I remember the sulky, parked with the shafts resting against the wall of the barn.

I never saw my grandfather ride, but I could see the pride in his eyes when he talked of racing. I remember the pride he must have seen in my eyes when he talked of racing, when he saw how much I loved to be with the horses. I didn't want to saddle them or ride them. I just wanted to be with them, to share their quietness.

One day he found me down at the stables as usual.

"You remind me of my dad," he said.

"The butcher?" I asked.

He laughed. "I suppose that's what your father told you. That's what he liked to think. My father did have some butcher's shops, but he also had a pub, a farm, a garage and a boat. He lived on the boat, a beautiful houseboat. He didn't like to stay still for long and, although the houseboat was moored, it never stopped moving. I don't suppose your dad told you that did he?"

He didn't, and it didn't matter. I felt an enormous sense of relief. I felt an immediate affinity with the man who couldn't stop moving.

LOCKUP

In the house we called him Brendan, but I knew he went by other names. The woman in the paper shop referred to him as Paddy but, back then, some people referred to every Irishman as Paddy. I met him in the street one time and his work mates called him Finn. In all the years we shared a house, that was the only time I saw him in company.

He was a solitary man. Even when I saw him working, he was alone. He was a paver. He reinstated the pavements after they'd been dug up to change a pipe or cable. A van dropped him off with a stack of paving stones, a pile of orange sand and the tools of his trade: a long wooden mallet; a bristle broom and a paver's lever.

He was a strong man. He could move a paving stone himself, walking it corner to corner. He'd learned to move slowly. There was no point hurrying in a job like his. Hurrying risked injury. Hurrying gave the wrong impression about the time needed to do good work.

Anyone who does a repetitive job learns to move slowly. Labourers are the slowest. Even after work, on the way home, he walked slowly. He'd stop to buy food for his dinner. Always the same: one King Edward potato, big enough to fill a pan; one thick slice of fatty steak.

Everyone who shared the house had a shelf in the fridge. His shelf was always empty.

He'd eat his breakfast in the café on the corner. The guy who drove the truck would deliver him a sandwich and a flask of tea for lunch. He'd eat his dinner at home. He'd put that big King Edward potato in a pan full of salty water and boil it ´til it burst. Then he'd throw the steak into a hot dry pan. It would soon yield enough fat to fry without burning, enough juice to gravy the potato.

We didn't talk much. He taught me not to bother him. He taught me gently, with silence and a nod. I learned to exchange no more than a word or two about the weather. Even so, he fascinated me and, I'm ashamed to say, I followed him quite a few times.

His life was mostly predictable: same café for breakfast; same butcher for meat; same greengrocer for his potato; same pub for the beer.

The pub was a place of beauty: carved wood; etched glass and mirrors; red velvet banquettes and chairs. The bar in the middle served three different rooms. The Guinness was said to be the best in town. No doubt, he'd remember when the barrel was wood, not metal.

Guinness was for slow people, people with time enough on their hands to wait for the first pour to settle before the glass was filled to the brim. Black red stout with a thick head of dense cream.

He'd always sit in the snug. I'd play bar billiards on the street side. Occasionally he'd see me and nod.

HORSE TRADER

Nobody knows where my father came from. He arrived on a boat with a brightly painted caravan and a small herd of horses. He was equally talented as a horse trader and a poker player.

He could listen to a horse and understand what it loved best. He could teach it what it needed.

He could listen to a man and learn his inner language. He could understand the subtle tics and twitches that laid bare his inner life.

Sometimes he would let a man win in order to beat him later. He would never play for more than a man could afford to lose. He told me that the keys to success are patience and silence.

Sometimes he chose to lose, as a way of giving a gift. He lost the caravan in a game of poker, to a man who couldn't afford to lose. He said he'd never before met a man with so much kindness, so little prejudice, who wanted a caravan so his children could go for holidays by the sea.

By then my father lived on a boat.

A DARK TEACHER

I switched religion at the age of fifteen, shifting allegiance from the roman church favoured by my mother to an altogether darker church favoured my father. I always thought he was agnostic but, when I reached fifteen, I discovered some hidden truths.

I realised that all the coolest kids I knew went to the church run by the queen of england and not by the vatican king. I learned that they didn't go for the teachings, because the queen's church had no pretentions when it came to nurturing the spirit. They went for the Friday night disco, and that's where I wanted to be.

I explained myself over the dinner table one evening. I told my mother that I wanted to compare churches before committing to hers. I told my father that I'd heard that the queen's church was a fake, that there was no connection with god. I told him I wanted to check out a godless life like his before committing either way.

"You've got me wrong, young man," he said. "But I like you're thinking. With your mother's permission I'd like to introduce you to my teacher."

The colour drained from my mother's face and she nervously fingered the crucifix she always wore round her neck.

She nodded her approval and my father broke out into a broad smile the likes of which I'd never before seen grace his usually solemn face.

"Go to the queen's church," he said. "And tell them you want to join. Better you don't mention the disco. Once they sign you up let me know."

Two weeks later I danced with the cool kids at the Friday disco. On the way home, I bumped into my father. "Now's the time," he said. "Let's go."

I followed him past our house, catching the twitch of the curtain, knowing my mother was watching from behind it.

He took me across the road to The Old Red Lion and into the men's bar. He ordered a pint of Guinness for himself and a half for me. I watched, mesmerised as the beer settled, a mysterious alchemy through which a seething chaos separated into a layer of black and a layer of white stillness.

"That," he said, "is called *transmutation*. Treated with reverence, this dark teacher will transmute loneliness into community, sadness into joy, ignorance into knowing. You'll never need another teacher."

When our people moved south to work in the mines, the homes we were promised were not yet built. No matter; we had our carts and benders, and our dogs assured us of a peaceful night's sleep wherever it was we laid our heads. Although walls of stone and doors that locked had their allure, we were in no hurry to shed the wheels and hoofs of our ancestors.

There was no shortage of work for every kind of hand. Diggers prepared the land for the railway, making its way up from the blast furnaces by the river. Diggers dug the trench that marked the line along which two rows of houses would be built. Masons built the houses with a yard big enough to raise a pig.

Each house had a privy and a wash room that drained into the trench between the rows. Soon, one of those houses would be ours. The stone came from the surrounding moorland. The land owners were more than happy to give the stone in exchange for land cleared and fit for grazing sheep.

I was a plater. My hands could coax a curve from a plate of iron. My hands could build the hull of ship. I learned my trade from my father, in the shipyard that took his life when he fell from a gantry. I was twelve when he died.

I took his place. It was the only way to avoid our family being evicted from the land around the shipyard.

My father built upwards, from the keel to the cope. I would build downwards. I would build a lift shaft deep into the earth until we cracked into the thick seam of iron ore that had brought a village to this empty land. I would build a hoist to take the diggers down.

I would build the iron barrows to haul the ore from the face to the surface.

We'd make a home for me to come back to after work, and our children would eat at a table. When the school was built, perhaps they'd learn to work with brain not brawn, perhaps they'd learn to count and write.

DIGGERS

I don't remember how I got the job, but one cold damp morning I found myself on a muddy strip hacked through the beautiful land from the north of Wales to the east coast of Scotland.

In the centre of that strip, a deep trench ready to receive a massive pipeline, one metre in diameter, big enough for a welder and his mate to travel inside on a buggy, fixing faults in the welds that had been picked up by remote controlled cameras and x-ray machines.

The welders, the crane drivers and the x-ray operators were the skilled end of the project. They were paid weekly on Thursdays; a sealed brown envelope with a cheque or cash, whichever they preferred.

I was at the other end, with the Irish, a curious crew of freckled men with big boned foreheads, deep eye sockets, and a constant good humour in the face of daily abuse. They welcomed me into their clan. Perhaps they could smell the Irish in me before I was even aware of it myself.

I coughed with them over the first cigarette of the day as the welders started the generators that belched clouds of black smoke into the crisp morning air.

We laboured at the dirty end of the project, without respect or decency, even from those who paid our wages, Irishmen themselves. Our work was to repair the land before returning it to the owner.

We were paid daily in cash, one day in arrears, out of the window of a battered old Range Rover. Our boss, a sub sub-contractor sat at the wheel with the cash box on his knee. His mate in the passenger seat held a sawn off shotgun on his lap.

The one with the money kept a book and noted down our name and the day of the week. The Irish lived on credit - not a lot, a few of hundred pounds, but enough to keep them trapped for ever.

We worked between two lines of bulldozers. The line ahead of us dragged the land with enormous claws, hauling out rocks and boulders. The line behind us had their buckets at the ready, ready to receive the rocks and boulders we rolled into them.

The bulldozer drivers were paid much better than us, but they were not allowed to stop until the break whistle was sounded.

That was the life on the Irish labour gang, this gang of sons and brothers, seduced to England with the promise of good wages - in debt, enslaved, treated like beasts of burden.

They all slept in one room in a flop house; sometimes in the back of the van if they were too drunk to climb the stairs to the room.

In the morning they'd fall out when the van doors were opened, some puking, all hungover, dragging their way through the morning until the van driver, William Blake, sounded the horn, called us to the van where pots of tea and steak sandwiches waited for us.

William Blake always parked the van a good half mile from where we worked. We'd carry on drinking tea, smoking and joking past the allotted break time.

The site foreman would have to walk down the site, banging on the sides of the van to get us to return to work.

"We're Irish," William Blake told me with a wink. "They think we're fucking stupid."

My father played piano in a local bar. He was lucky to have some work; there was little to be had when the last pit closed. Back then things ended properly. Now nothing ever seems to end.

The last day at the pit was announced a month in advance. The last barrow of iron ore was hoisted to the surface while the mayor and his cronies clapped.

The men lined up for the last pay packet, a small brown envelope with the total written on the outside. If there was quibbling to be done it had to be done before the envelope was opened.

Nobody quibbled that day. A full week's wages and a month more in compensation was cash enough to tie their tongues. Wives and mothers waited at the gate and left the men with just enough for one night of serious drinking.

My father never worked in the pit. He didn't want to risk his fingers. Friends at school said he was the last real gypsy. I didn't agree because we lived in a house. But then I noticed he never stayed home for long, just long enough for a pot of tea and half a cigarette with my mother. It might not have been much, but she was always happy to see him.

One day he gave me a pony, a pony in a paddock. The pony had a railway carriage for shelter and some bales of hay. My mother found me a saddle and a halter.

After a day in the field with the pony we understood each other. She showed me where she wanted to go and I looked ahead for the dangers she couldn't hear.

In that part of the world a pony was a ticket to the hunt. On the last Saturday of the month, just before daybreak, pony took me to the manor.

I was shooed to the back with the riff raff while the drunken toffs at the front whooped and hollered each time they caught sight of the poor mangy fox that would lose its life to the hound pack that morning.

At the end of the hunt, we returned to the manor for hot chocolate and rum. I was surprised to find my father waiting for me there. He'd never met me from anything before. But he took pony by the halter and paraded us like the proud father he never was.

The lord of the manor leered at me but addressed my father. "You play piano in the Miner's Arms don't you?"

Father nodded; he wasn't one for words.

"Would you come in and play for us, we're having a bit of a party?"

Father nodded. He slapped pony on the flank and sent us on our way.

That night he won the manor stables in a game of poker. It came complete with ten hunt horses and twenty foxhound couples. There was a house for the groom and a house for us.

We moved in the following day. My father agreed to let the lord use the horses and hounds as long as he paid for their upkeep and provided coal to warm our house.

THE POET

Everyone knew the poet. Everyone had paid a shilling to read a poem. Everyone was surprised that a shilling was only enough to read, but not to keep the scrap of cardboard on which the poem was written. Nobody knew if he really wrote it. Nobody knew if he wrote more, or if that was the only poem he ever wrote.

It didn't matter. He was known as the poet, and that was how he made his money; the money he used to buy cigarettes that yellowed his beard and stained his fingers brown. The money he used to buy cheap liquor that scarred his liver and turned his voice to a growl. That's what poets did back then. They smoked, they drank, they growled, and they made money from their poems.

The poet was killed one night, beaten to death by one of the drunks. They say the poet died because he drank the whiskers. They say he was beaten to death by a drunk who wanted the whiskers. Beaten to death for the last mouthful of cheap liquor and the threads of spit from all the other drinkers.

QUEEN

I once saw a queen. She drove slowly by in a big black car with tall windows. She smiled and waved in such a way that everyone thought she was smiling at them.

She didn't stay long – perhaps just a minute as she drove down our road. We'd all been told to stand outside, and smile and wave flags when she went by.

It was nice that she came because the council washed the road with bleach. The council painted our front door and window as well. The council hung bunting the full length of the road. It was the first time I'd seen bunting. My mother said she'd seen it once before, when the queen got married.

We had to take in all our toys and furniture apart from the table. All the mothers made cakes and sandwiches to put on their table. We couldn't touch them until the queen had gone.

I felt sorry for her; they wouldn't stop and let her out for cake. My mother had made her a Battenberg cake especially.

The men were told not to smoke. When the queen's car turned into our road, my father put out his cigarette and tucked it behind his ear for later. We smiled and waved our flags.

When her car left, we ate sandwiches and cakes. My mother drank some sherry and got tipsy. My father went to the pub. We brought our toys back out and played until the sun went down. Next day the council came and took away the bunting.

He ran a mile or two before he caught up with the dog, a lurcher running through the streets of the city; barking, a searching needy bark, not threatening but calling for attention, a red and white banner tied to her collar, flapping in the wind as she ran.

He called as he ran, "Hey girl, what is it? Don't run, girl. Just stop a moment and talk with me, perhaps I can help."

His words finally got to her and she stopped, turned to face him, sat and waited for him to catch up - he, red faced and breathless by now.

He slowed his pace to walking, didn't want to frighten her now she'd settled. He walked the last ten paces, hand outstretched, reassuring, "good girl, well done. it's ok, let me see what you've got there."

As he got closer, he could see better. Tied to her collar, the red and white banner, a brass name disk and a key with a wooden tag.

CRABS' LEGS

I held her hand as we watched the fishing coble, pushed up the beach by the high tide. The fishermen, wearing waders, jumped ashore. One ran up the beach to fetch the tractor and trailer. The others steadied the boat against the beat of the sea.

"As a kid I'd always come here with my friends. For sixpence we could buy a pound of crabs' legs wrapped in newspaper. We'd crunch them and suck out the juice and flesh, spitting the splinters of shell into the sand beneath the sea wall."

"What happened to the rest of the crab?" she asked.

"The fisher wives dressed them and sold them to the holiday makers."

"They dressed them? How do you dress a crab?" she asked.

"They'd cook them in boiling water. Then they'd crack open the body..."

"You call that 'dressed'? I'd call that killed."

"They killed them first. Then they pulled away the base of the shell and twisted off the legs for poor people like us.

"They'd pull out the mouth and stomach and throw it away, along with the dead men's fingers. Then they'd scrape out the meat, separate the brown from the white, pack it back into the freshly washed shell. Then they'd carefully crack the claws with a hammer and arrange everything on a white ceramic plate to display in the cold cabinet."

"You people are weird!" she said. "That's not dressed. At best that's undressed."

DEATH IN A TRENCH

In our family, when a funeral cortege passes by, we hold the lapel of our jacket between thumb and forefinger until the coffin is out of sight. Nobody told me to do it and nobody explained why. I did it because I saw my father do it and it seemed like the right thing to do.

That's what I did that morning, when all the horns on the site sounded in unison. That's what I did for one minute when the horns stopped and the site fell silent. After a minute the welders started up their generators and the warning bells rang on the cranes. One minute's silence to mark a man's death.

He only had a first name. He didn't have papers. He had friends but they were as nameless and homeless as he. I know how he died, crushed between steel and earth.

His job that day was to stand on the pipe, holding the chain, pushing the pipe from the sides of the trench, as the cranes lowered it into its final resting place. That was his final resting place too. No point reporting the death of a man without a name, a man without a home.

I'd done that job too; I knew the danger. But if you were told to do it, you couldn't say no. No was the same as get your things and go.

Four cranes lifting four sections of pipeline, welded together on the side of the trench. It saved a lot of time compared to welding two meters down in the trench.

The cranes weren't designed for that lift. Their alarm bells rang as they teetered forward on their tracks. The crane drivers were well paid for the risk. They could afford to buy a house. They could go home, sit in an armchair, think of the man who died that day.

THE KEY

Every day he came in, always at 4.30 in the afternoon. I guess he waited for the school kids to finish buying sweets and vapes before they headed to the park to fix their moods before going home.

He'd shuffle around the shop, always in the same direction, counter-clockwise, counter-intuitive, starting at the pasta section and finishing at the magazines.

Everybody else started at the magazines and either stopped there and paid, or headed to the chilled cabinet for milk or a pork pie, only to be drawn into some random purchase on the way back to the till. That was how the shop was designed.

Although he always shuffled in the same direction, his browsing wasn't predictable. Sometimes he would spend five minutes inspecting the pastas. There were curly ones, spiral ones, straight ones, tubes, ears, dolphins and shells. But he never bought pasta.

Sometimes he browsed the soups. There was a whole section dedicated to Warhol – classic soups from Campbell that needed some skill to prepare. There were easier brands, ready to heat straight from the can. But he never bought a can of soup.

Occasionally, he bought a packet of powdered soup; salty chicken with bits of broken vermicelli. He never bought more than that, even if he always gave the impression he would. More often he left empty handed, offering a brief nod on his way out the door.

One day, I couldn't hold myself back any longer when he came to pay. "What is it you're really looking for?" I asked.

He was taken aback, touched by the question. Perhaps just touched that someone paid him some attention. He stared at me. For a good minute he stared, his eyes soft, glistening with tears, searching for an answer that was worthy of the question.

"Thank you so much for asking," he said. "Nobody asked me that before. Do you really want to know?"

The shop was empty. The school rush was over. The next rush would be at six, when the workers came home, bought their lottery tickets, tins of beer, packets of snacks and cigarettes, ready for a night in front of the television.

I nodded yes.

"I'm looking for a key."

He was silent. I waited for more but he said no more, as if he'd said all that was necessary to satisfy the question.

"What kind of key? A key to what?" I asked, when I realized he wouldn't be more forthcoming.

"To my soul," he said.

THE CODE

I wouldn't normally turn on a brother in arms; it was against everything I'd been raised to defend. Amongst our people we didn't have a god to scare us. We didn't have any idea of a heaven or hell.

For our people dead was dead. There was no reckoning, no judging, no weighing. Nothing to carry over. Dust to dust and no mention of a spirit or soul.

We did have a code of conduct but, we didn't have any external method of enforcing it.

'Act as if your father is watching,' is all I was ever told. But I was told in a moment of such awareness that the suggestion seemed to infiltrate every cell of my brain, seemed to leave its mark whichever way my thinking turned.

'Act as if your father is watching.' That's how I lived my life.

Although I lived by the code, I only ever remembered those words a few of times as I grew from child into man, buried my father, carried his blade.

One time, I almost stole an apple from a neighbour's tree. Another time, I almost kicked a small dog that barked at me.

Once, I almost shouted at an old lady who stopped and fumbled with her bag on the path in front of me.

When I turned on my brother in arms, I not only turned on him but on myself, my father, my grandfather, and the code itself - passed from man to man, from forever ago.

He knew it, of course, knew the force that froze me in my tracks. It must have frozen him once as well, as he was one of our people. But he had the advantage; he had already broken the code, and nothing would hold him back from the crime he was eager to commit. Nothing but me.

I couldn't fight him face to face; we were both good with a blade, but he'd already killed a man and he would be my first. I backed down, sheathed my blade, gave him my power. He took it, turned his back on me, walked away pumped with pride while I scraped the dirt from the sole of my shoe and threw a hex. Next day he was dead, in a trench. Crushed between steel and earth.

It isn't easy to follow a slow man without looking like you're loitering. Brendan was slow but he never loitered. For most people he was invisible, hidden beneath a tweed jacket, cloth cap and loose corduroy trousers.

It was Sunday. On Sunday, Brendan went to morning mass. On Sunday, Brendan polished his shoes and wore his Sunday shirt. During the week he wore a vest beneath his jacket. On Sunday he washed his vest before mass and wore his Sunday shirt.

Sometimes I'd follow him until he disappeared into church. I would have followed him in but I was a lapsed catholic and the guilt I carried was too big to get through the door.

I woke up late; I'd drunk too much, in a pub that served beer straight from a wooden barrel. With beer that smooth, you could drink three pints before you realised your mistake. Three pints is one too many and one too many leads to many more.

I woke with a dry mouth and a headache. I swallowed two aspirin with black coffee and left the house. I had a lunch date I couldn't afford to miss.

I walked past the church and slowed my pace. In the distance Brendan turned into a street that led to nowhere but a row of garages, mostly abandoned since everyone built a car port in front of their house.

I should have stopped and retreated. I should have remembered lunch. I should have known better than to follow a man who wanted to remain invisible. The big calloused hand that gripped my arm told me all that in a moment.

"What the fuck do you want?" Brendan asked. His eyes holding me with as much fury as his hand.

"Nothing. I'm sorry."

"Who do you work for?"

"What do you mean? I'm not working, I'm studying. I thought you knew that."

"Why do you keep following me?"

I felt so much shame as I thought of all the stupid answers I could give. Because I like you. Because you fascinate me. Because you remind me of someone. Because I'm nosy.

"I don't know. I really don't know. Please just let me go and I promise I'll never to do it again."

Brendan manhandled me into the lockup. "Sit."

He pushed me down into an old armchair and pulled up a footstool to sit and face me. I instinctively reached for my cigarettes.

"I wouldn't do that if I were you," he said.

I paused, cigarette hanging from my lips.

"Take a look around you."

I saw nothing but boxes stacked from floor to ceiling. Identical boxes; old, stained, brown cardboard boxes filling all the space apart from the little area in the middle where we sat.

"What am I looking at?"

"Frangex; gelignite from Enfield. A ton of the fucking stuff weeping away in here. Somewhere there's a box of detonators but I can't remember where."

"What the fuck!" I said, getting up from my armchair. But Brendan wasn't having any of it and pushed me back into the seat.

"You can't go. You've got to help me get rid of this. It's your karma."

"Karma? What the fuck do you mean by karma? You're a fucking catholic, not a buddhist."

"I met a woman who told me about karma. And, anyway, I'm not a catholic, I only tried that when the drink didn't work. And I'm not a buddhist either, I follow Kashmiri Shaivism."

Brendan's words utterly silenced me and I felt peaceful and happy like never before. I gazed at him. He seemed to have lost his stoop. His Sunday shirt glowed white. His green eyes were soft and kind.

"Where did you learn about Kashmiri Shaivism?" I asked.

"From the woman in the corner shop."

I couldn't help but laugh. "The cigarette shop, are you fucking serious, you learned about Kashmiri Shaivism from the woman in the cigarette shop?"

"She's my teacher now. She told me how to free myself from my karma. She told me I had to find an ally, someone clever like you, someone who understood how this country worked. She said I just had to wait and he'd come into my life. And here you are. Now help me get rid of this stuff before it blows us up."

Night whispers

"Things can get out of a black hole, both to the outside, and possibly, to another universe. So, if you feel you are in a black hole, don't give up. There's a way out."

Professor Stephen Hawking, 2008

I couldn't say for sure if I slept and dreamed or lay awake and dreamed but, by the time my mother switched off the light in our cabin, I was already in another world, able to hear her wish me goodnight but unable to find the piece of mind to respond.

It was our first night on a Spanish train but I already knew the language of the engine; the same as the English one that brought us from our home to the ferry. In England, the engine driver answered every one of my questions as we waited for the boiler to build a head of steam in time to leave.

Now, I could feel the pressure dropping in the boiler. I could hear the sound of the pistons as their brief reach and return became more arduous. I knew the engineer would fill the oil can, walk along the side of the engine, refill the reservoirs on each piston.

I heard a whisper from the furnace, a hoarse call from the fire to the stoker to bring more coal. "Patience", he whispered back. "Let me clear out the clinkers and cinders before I fill you afresh."

Behind him, two men, blackened with coal dust, streaked with sweat, shovelled coal from the back to the front of the tender, ready for the stoker to feed the fire.

I felt the pressure build, the shrill hiss of the relief valve as the boiler reached its limit, the soft clank of bronze on bronze as the engine driver pulled a lever to open the valves that fed steam to the pistons. The train returned to full power.

I smelled tobacco smoke drifting down past the carriage windows as the engine crew settled into a rest, wiping the sweat and coal dust from their faces.

I heard my mother's breath slow down, hover a moment before exhaling, release a deep spontaneous sigh and settle into the soft and regular breath of deep sleep. If mother was asleep, I knew my sisters were already sleeping.

I turned to my side and pushed the pillow away. I let my ear sink into the mattress. I listened through the mattress, into the bed frame, into the wooden floor, into the creaking girders that made up the bogie.

I could hear iron wheels on iron rails, the rhythm of expansion joints, the crunch of wooden sleepers on a bed of gravel. I could hear steel ball bearings in bronze ball races, the rattle of safety chains between the carriages.

Somewhere, in the dark kingdom of the night, the train came to rest and a community of sleepers shared a dream.

I heard an invisible work force loading coal; filling tanks with fresh water; greasing axles; tapping wheels; listening for the sound that betrayed a fracture; unhitching and shunting carriages; building two trains out of one; introducing a new engine to the section that would take us to Barcelona while the rest of the carriages journeyed south.

My mother's friend met us from the ferry. "You'll like Beryl," she´d said, and I did, right from the start. She was clever like my mother and they talked about things I didn't understand; intangible things like time and space and knowledge.

We all climbed into a big old car driven by Joan, a friend of Beryl. Mother and Beryl sat up front with Joan, on a long bench seat. My sisters and I sat in the back. The luggage had to go on the roof; the boot wouldn't open because of an enormous cylinder attached to the door.

"What's that?" I asked. "A boiler, like on a steam train?"

Joan laughed. "Better than a boiler; it's a little factory that makes gas out of almond shells. It's difficult to get gasoline so we have to make do with what we have."

He showed me the pipes that fed gas to the engine, but warned me away from touching the cylinder, hot from the almond husks smouldering inside.

"This is an American car," he said. "It will run on anything."

And run it did, but not very well. I could feel the engine struggle with its meagre meal of carbon monoxide and air and it took a mile or two to find its rhythm. The poor car was carrying a lot of weight with the six of us and all our luggage.

When my father left for his yearly trip to Africa, I watched my mother pack those trunks. They were so big I was sure we were leaving forever. I feared I'd never spend another holiday in the caravan my father had parked in a field near Weymouth. It was brightly decorated when he bought it from a Romani horse trader, but he painted it green so it wouldn't attract too much attention.

Before we left, I searched my treasure box for the plug of boxwood I always brought back from the caravan. I carved it myself using the knife my father brought me from one of his trips. From my high bunk, I could look out through a hole and watch the stars. I don't know why it was there. Father said it was a spyhole. I called it the wormhole. If I was lucky, I might catch sight of Pleiades. On windy nights I'd fit the plug to keep the breeze from my cricking my neck.

I ran that wooden plug, polished from so much love, between my fingers as we drove towards the mountains.

The car began to struggle and Joan pulled over to the side of the road. He called me out to watch and, with the engine still running, he opened a stop cock from a small tank mounted on the side of the bonnet. The engine woke up and found a joyful rhythm I hadn't heard before.

"A little gasoline," Joan said. "A precious aphrodisiac for an old girl like this."

I got back into the car with the word *aphrodisiac* rolling around in my mind. I didn't know exactly what it was, but I liked the feel of the word and I liked what it did for the engine as we drove higher into the mountains.

The climb settled into level road again and we passed by a beautiful town built into the hillside. I struggled to hear what Beryl was saying to my mother but I'd heard the word *philosopher* and I sharpened my hearing enough to hear the names *Ramon Llull* and *Jorge Luis Borges* over the song of the engine.

My mother once told me that a philosopher was a lover of wisdom and now, as we sped through orchards of olive trees, I knew I wanted to be a lover of wisdom.

When Joan stopped the car again, it was at a lay-by from where we could gaze over terraces of olive trees to the sea. He adjusted the gasoline supply to the engine.

"Just a little now but there's not enough heat left in the almonds to do without."

He pointed toward the horizon. "Look, nothing but sea until Barcelona." And then he led our eyes along the coastline to a village. "And, over there, Deia, the most beautiful place on the island. Welcome to my world."

As we drove into the village, it really did feel like Joan's world. Everybody knew him and he stopped many times in the middle of the road to chat with friends. When he stopped outside the house mother had rented for us, his friends arrived to help us carry our luggage in. None would accept the money mother offered. Beryl invited us to lunch and then continued in the car with Joan.

The house was so cool and quiet that I just wanted to lie on the floor. Mother suggested I do that upstairs as there was too much activity in the entrance room where I lay.

I followed her and we chose me a bedroom, at the back of the house with a view onto a garden full of lemon trees.

I was so happy to lie on that big bed with its four spiral turned posts, and a canopy to pull down against the light. I still missed the caravan but this wasn't so bad.

I dug into my pocket for the boxwood plug. I felt safe. I rolled onto my side. I could see light shining through a hole in the bed post. The boxwood plug fitted perfectly and I knew I'd found another wormhole. I removed the plug and looked through the hole into our seaside caravan.

I could see my bunk. I could see the bedding folded in a neat pile, just as I left it. I could see my favourite glass marble sitting on top. I brought it from our home in St Albans. Leaving it there felt like leaving a little piece of me to come back to.

I slept and dreamed I was sleeping on my bunk. When mother woke me for lunch I was confused. The heat and sounds and smells outside soon reminded me where I was. We walked to Beryl's house and I was struck with how kind and friendly people were. They were not like that in St Albans.

Beryl had a husband and four children and we all gathered around a long table on the terrace for lunch. Beryl's son, William, was put next to me. He was more or less the same age and I discovered that we were going to summer school together.

It was lucky we liked each other as there wasn't any choice. In our house everyone had a say but, in this house, Beryl's husband was the boss.

Summer school turned out to be just the two of us and a tutor, a friend of William's father. He wanted us to study the Bible.

I told him, "In our family, we don't believe in religion. My parents are intellectuals and communists. They believe in science and facts. My mother says religion is the opiate of the masses."

Our tutor laughed. "You'd do well to keep that opinion to yourself in this country. Don't read the Bible literally. Think of it as mythology, an attempt to understand creation and creativity through allegory."

I was willing to work with that, but I trusted my parents' deference to science.

Each day we had to read one chapter, beginning with the book of Genesis, and then write something about it.

Our tutor wasn't really bothered what we wrote, he had his own writing to keep him busy. He was working on a play.

The first chapter was easy enough, a brief description of a week in the life of God.

It was a busy week during which he created heaven and earth; the sun, the moon and the stars; night and day; land and sea; every kind of plant and every kind of animal. He then made a man and a woman who looked like himself.

I found that interesting. If the man and woman looked like God, was God the same size as us? And did the man and woman look the same as each other?

I knew not to trouble our tutor with my questions so I carried them with me as William and I were freed from our duty. After class we went to William's house for a snack. They called it *berenar*. There were always big slabs of brown bread rubbed with crushed garlic and tomato, smothered in olive oil, sprinkled with sea salt. We could help ourselves to slices of hard cheese, dry ham and olives. It didn't take long for me to adapt to the food, everything tasted so delicious.

Beryl's husband always joined us. I loved to listen to him talking with our mothers. He'd ask William and me what we'd read, but he didn't really listen to us. He was a clever man with a head full of ideas and stories and had little time for our opinions. He said the Bible was one of many creation myths, just another way to understand how we, the people, found ourselves on our beautiful planet in a vast and unfathomable universe.

I learned from him that God had a name, *Yahweh Elohim* – which meant the god who created everything that exists.

When William was with his friends, he excluded me. I didn't mind, I had plenty to think about and I didn't really want to run with boys when I didn't know what they were saying.

I was free to walk home on my own. People were very open and I learned to nod my head by raising my chin, or say '*adeu*'. When I discovered '*adeu*' translated as 'go to god' I just nodded my head.

I removed the plug from the wormhole in my bed and looked from inside our caravan onto a place I loved - a wild meadow, vibrant with spring flowers and pollenating insects, horse chestnut trees swaying in a gentle breeze. In the distance, a calm sea and a clear blue sky.

Mother woke me and we all walked down to Cala Deia, a little rocky cove. The sea was too cold for me. I was glad. Even though people were swimming, it was very difficult to get in and out of the water as the stones were smooth and slippery. I preferred the sand of Weymouth Beach.

I was so happy to finish our first week of school. I was unimpressed by the Bible.

It was a childish explanation of how the world was created, and God was such a selfish person. He created a man and a woman who looked just like him. He called them Adam and Eve. He imprisoned them in a garden called Eden.

He created thousands of plants and animals and then asked Adam to think of names for them all. He planted a tree of knowledge and told them they'd die if they took from it.

When Adam and Eve chose knowledge over ignorance, God thew them out of the garden of Eden and cursed them to have a difficult life. They went on to have lots of children and grandchildren. When God saw them suffering human difficulties in line with his curse, he decided to drown them all.

My respect for my godless parents deepened and I vowed to eat from the tree of knowledge no matter how much difficulty it might cause me.

Neither our tutor nor William's father wanted to talk about any of this, so I stopped asking questions during *berenar* and just listened. I realised that none of the adults at the table believed the Bible; they were more interested in why our ancestors invented such strange stories.

William's father lowered his voice and I knew he was about to share something important between the grownups.

I took the boxwood plug between my fingers and imagined a wormhole through which I could listen.

"I have been corresponding with an amazing man called Gordon Wasson, the most civilized American I know. He and his wife, Natacha, have been researching the use of hallucinogenic mushrooms in ancient cultures around the world. He sent me some Mexican mushrooms. Beryl and I ate some and experienced incredible transcendental visions.

"I cannot but agree with Gordon, that the reason our ancestors wrote stories about gods and heaven and hell was due to their experiences with these magical mushrooms."

He passed a paper bag to my mother. "These may be the *ambrosia* referred to by the ancient Greeks, the food of the gods, the plant of immortality. Take a handful, you might have a quiet moment one morning."

Mother peered inside, sniffed and smiled before reaching into the bag.

That night, when I knew my mother and sisters were sleeping, as if guided by another self, I went down into the kitchen and found the glass jar where mother had put the mushrooms. I took a couple and, without compunction, chewed them and swallowed them down with a glass of water.

Back in my bed, I drew down the canopy. My muscles relaxed and a wave of warmth flowed through my body and mind. I was sitting in my own garden of Eden, with its meadow of wild flowers, hedges, bushes and trees and views to a sandy beach and the sea.

I could see strange sparkles in the air; whorls, auras and other momentary tricks of light. I knew they were wormholes, opening and closing too quickly for me to peer inside.

I found my boxwood plug and held it tightly in my fist. Some of the wormholes settled. I peered into one, into the garden of Eden.

I saw three people hand in hand. I knew one of them was God, one was Adam and one was Eve. They were naked, but nothing differentiated man from woman, human from god.

Two mushrooms grew at their feet. One bestowed health and longevity, the other knowledge and differentiation.

I peered into another wormhole and I could see deep into space. I could see immense movements of gasses and matter. I could see condensation as gasses became solid. I could see differentiation as planets separated from space, and water separated from rock.

Through another wormhole I could see rock become lichen, lichen become earth, earth become plant and plant become tree. I could see a mycelium web communicating the knowledge of differentiation to all things. Mushrooms sprouted, each one proclaiming its purpose.

Through another wormhole I could see creatures form and adapt. Some swam within a vast ocean. Smaller ones discovered rivers and streams. Some budded limbs or grew slither muscles when they found mud banks on the side of the river. Some grew feathers or fur to protect against the cold while others chilled their blood to protect against the heat.

Now I was looking again into the biblical garden of Eden.

Adam and Eve had eaten the mushroom of knowledge and differentiation. God was furious because he had lost his ignorant companions. He chose loneliness over equality. He threw them out of the garden of Eden so they could no longer eat the mushroom of immortality.

Now I knew I would choose knowledge over immortality and I would dedicate my life to finding a way to peer back in time through wormholes and, perhaps one day, to travel through them to distant worlds.

Other books by Howard Evans:

A Myofascial Approach to Thai Massage, 2009

STILL, a magical novel, 2019

LOVE SEX DEATH, a book of short stories, 2021

Printed in Great Britain
by Amazon

11530616R00108